A Victim in the Village

THE REBECCA ORANGE CASTLE COZY MYSTERY SERIES
BOOK TWO

VALERIE BRANDY

Contents

CHAPTER

One

"YOU'RE GOING TO LOVE THIS," Maggie says, taking my hand as she pulls me through the Village of Atwood. "All the vendors for the Foundation Festival will be there, and *we* get to be the first to sample what they're bringing to the festival!"

We round a corner, revealing a quaint street bordered by pastel buildings. Brightly colored flowers vine their way up the stucco walls. The sweet scent of honeysuckle fills the air. I've only lived in Monrovia for a short period of time, but it already feels like home. The country is small and I haven't had a chance to see much of it, but the Village of Atwood is a jewel in its crown. Beside me, my giant Tibetan Mastiff— Joe — struggles to keep up, panting at the brisk pace we're keeping.

"I think Joe's been indulging a little *too* much in the snacks here," I tell Maggie. "He's gained about ten pounds since we moved to Monrovia."

Maggie waves a hand in the air as if numbers don't matter. "He looks great to me. Very handsome. What's ten extra pounds when you already weigh over two-hundred?" She says brightly.

"A few more years in Monrovia and I'll be saying the same thing about *myself*," I laugh out loud.

We pass the fountain that serves as the center of the town square, the sound of the flowing water creating a peaceful ambiance in the village. Closed windows and drawn curtains mark the apartments circling the courtyard. Almost everyone is asleep this early. We've come with a purpose, and we're beating the crowds.

"So what exactly did the Duke want us to do?" I ask, my stomach flipping a little at the mention of Jack— the Duke of Atwood— who also happens to be my employer. *And* who happens to be very charming. And obnoxiously attractive. And one of my favorite people to spend time around since we solved a murder together just a few weeks ago.

"He wants us to sample the vendor offerings for the Foundation Festival! It's the world's best job," Maggie smiles at me. The knowing look in her eyes makes me think she suspects me of feeling something for the Duke. As if shopping could throw her off my trail, I stop at a table outside the teapot store, examining a China plate. "Jocelyn, the owner of *Cafe de Flore*, has agreed to let everyone set up sample booths on the patio outside her shop," Maggie continues. "The castle opened up the opportunity, and the entire village applied; but the castle only selected a few top vendors. These are the best of the best. It's our job today to make sure what they're offering is up to par."

I set down the China plate and start walking again, following Maggie down the cobblestone street. Joe sneezes next to me, his enormous nose spraying snot across my leg. "Guess everyone takes this Foundation Festival pretty seriously, then?" I ask Maggie.

"The Foundation Festival is a big deal for the village," Maggie says, taking on the tone she uses when she's about to give me a history lesson. Due to the fact I'm still learning about my new home, I get these lessons a lot. *Look serious*, I think to myself. I glance down at Joe, who's seated on his haunches as if he's in training class. Maggie stops and points at a statue that stands on the street corner.

It's a marble carving of a beautiful woman in robes holding a basket of bread. "Legend has it that Monrovia was founded by a woman," Maggie continues, pointing at the statue. "She was the leader of her tribe, and even in times of drought, she always made sure her people never went hungry. According to the myth, her village was dying because of the greed of evil men who kept all the food for themselves."

"I feel like I may have dated the descendants of these men," I laugh, thinking about Travis.

"Tell me about it," Maggie agrees. "Monrosha was starving and gave her last piece of bread to a child in the village. Because of the act of kindness, the bread multiplied, becoming fifty loaves. Upon seeing what had happened, the villagers rose up and made the woman their new Queen. Monrosha is the reason Monrovia exists today. The Foundation Festival celebrates the history of our country, which is, I say proudly, very female."

I stare up at Monrosha's face. Her cheekbones are high, her eyes closed. There's a determined expression etched into her features. "That's a history to be proud of," I tell Maggie.

"And, as you can see, our history also has to do with food!" Maggie points at the basket in the marble statue's hands, emphasizing the bread within.

"Oh, *that's* why we both eat so much," I exclaim. "It's not because we're gluttonous! It's because we're *patriotic*."

"Exactly," Maggie agrees, offering me a salute. "Happy to do anything to support my country. Some of the vendors today have food, so—"

"So the Duke was being generous giving us this assignment," I nod.

Maggie looks away sheepishly. "When I said the *Duke*

wanted us to test the vendors today, what I really meant was that he approved what *I* wanted. Which was to eat croissants and drink coffee."

"Sounds like Jack," I laugh.

Maggie links her arm in mine. We continue walking down the cobblestone alley, making a turn onto a narrow road. "He said I could bring anyone on staff, and of course I chose you."

"When you said we'd be going for an early breakfast, I had no idea it would be such an adventure," I tell her.

We stop at our destination— *Cafe de Flore* — one of my favorite places to eat in Monrovia. It's part cafe, part bookshop, and the space features flowers throughout.

"Hey, when you're my friend, there's nothing *but* adventure!" Maggie says. She pushes open the front door. Joe follows her, and the three of us make our way into the familiar, book-lined storefront of *Cafe de Flore.* But we don't get very far before a bark escapes Joe's lips, followed by an emergency whine.

There, in the middle of the floor—

Is a body.

A *dead* body.

Joe whimpers, running to hide behind me.

"You were saying about adventure?" I ask Maggie dryly.

She gasps, covering her mouth and taking a step back. "Not again," she says, shaking her head. "This can't be happening *again*. It's not possible!"

I point at the slumped figure on the floor, a pool of blood gathering beneath his frame. "I think he would disagree."

CHAPTER
Two

"WE SHOULD CALL THE POLICE," Maggie says, looking at me with tears in her eyes. She leans over the body, staring at the man's face. Dried blood marks his forehead—he must have died from a blow to the head. Beside him, a chair's been tipped over. On one of its sturdy wooden legs, dark blood seems to mark the chair as the murder weapon. "Oh my gosh, I know him," Maggie says, wiping her eyes. "So do you."

I bend down, getting a better look at the figure on the floor. It takes me a second to place the scratchy beard and beady eyes, but then I recognize him as the man who runs the newsstand in the village courtyard. He's the one who writes negative press on Jack— the Duke of Atwood. I'm ashamed to consider how many of his gossip magazines I've purchased.

"Rodrigo. He runs the gossip magazine you're always buying," Maggie says in a hushed tone, addressing my love of glad rags head-on, without a hint of shame.

"I don't buy them *that* often—"

Maggie gives me a skeptical look, then moves on. "He owns the tabloid stand too. He was the one who started the bad-boy bachelor rumor about the Duke of Atwood years ago, and we can also thank him for labeling us the 'castle of death' when Phillipe was killed. He's a terrible liar. His reports drive the Duke crazy."

"I don't think he'll be doing that anymore," I say, shaking my head. I point at the tipped chair beside him, motioning to the blood on its leg. "Someone hit him over the head with the chair. There's our murder weapon."

Maggie takes out her cell phone and dials the Monrovian police, her hands trembling. As I watch her, my stomach churns, acid rising in my throat. I swallow hard, pushing the feeling down. I can't believe this is happening again. Another murder. I glance down at Joe, who's sitting at my feet as if he's trying to protect me from meeting the same fate as Rodrigo. He whimpers, pushing his soft back into my legs. I stare at the body on the floor. The man who had once been a thorn in the Duke's side is now just a lifeless form, lying cold and still.

Maggie's voice is a blur. She's talking to the Monrovian Police, but I can't make out what she's saying. Instead, I take another look at Rodrigo's body. On closer inspection, I notice something strange— a slip of paper clutched tightly in his right hand.

Carefully, so as not to disturb the crime scene any further, I pry open his fingers and extract the page. It's a typed news-paper lead that's been ripped apart— as if someone pulled it from his lifeless hands. Whoever ripped the article away took the body of text with them, but the article title survived. It reads:

"The crown doesn't belong on his head."

A chill runs down my spine as I read those words. What could they possibly mean? Are they referencing the Duke? There's not many people in Atwood who wear a crown upon their head. Did Rodrigo unearth something that would hurt the Duke? If so, did it lead to his demise?

Maggie finishes her call and turns to me, her face pale. "They're on their way." She glances down at the paper I'm holding and gasps slightly, almost as if she can sense it's nothing but bad news. "What's that?"

I hand over the page without saying a word. Her eyes scan over it quickly, then widen in shock.

"The crown doesn't belong on his head?" She reads aloud, shivering. "He couldn't possibly be talking about—"

"The Duke?" I counter. "Do you know many other people around here who wear crowns on their heads? I guess I might qualify, if a shower cap counts."

"The Duke invited… Rodrigo… to be a part of the Foundation Festival," Maggie says, piecing the words together one at a time like she's stringing pearls on a thread. "I told him it was a bad idea, but he said part of being Royal is reaching out to those you don't like. Even those who criticize you. I thought maybe this would give Rodrigo a chance to see who the Duke really is, but all this time, he's been sitting on a lead. I bet he was planning to publish it during the Foundation Festival. To create as much drama as possible to sell more magazines."

"Well, he's certainly created drama," I say, stepping away from Rodrigo's limp body.

As we wait for the police to arrive, Joe curls up by my feet, his tail whipping back and forth to signal his distress. Suddenly, our taste-testing for the Foundation Festival seems trivial in comparison to what lies ahead. Whoever killed Rodrigo must have had a reason to want to stop his story from getting out. What did Rodrigo know, and who would be willing to murder for it?

CHAPTER
Three

THE FLASHING blue lights from Monrovian police cruisers paint the cobblestones in a surreal dance of color as I watch them cordon off the area. We're standing outside *Cafe de Flore*, staring down the woman I've now come to know as Officer Basilier. She's all business. Petite yet imposing, she moves through the scene with an air of authority that seems to silence even the whispering bystanders who stare at us from across the street.

"Step back, please," she commands, her voice cutting through the murmuring crowd, smooth as a knife through butter. Her sharp, focused eyes take in every detail as she surveys the unfortunate sight before us.

Photographers snap pictures from all angles, their camera flashes stark against the cobblestone. In the wake of Rodrigo's death, it seems other reporters haven't wasted a second filling the void. When the Police arrived, they insisted Maggie, Joe, and I exit *Cafe de Flore*— the scene of the crime— and stand on the walkway outside the shop instead. At the time the street was empty, but now, reporters crowd into a line like ants. Police tape across the street keeps them at bay. Still, a chorus of shouting emerges as two officers wheel out a gurney. On top sits Rodrigo's body, covered in a white sheet. They load him into an unmarked van as if he's a delivery.

"Rebecca? Rebecca Orange?" Officer Basilier's voice snaps me out of my thoughts. Beside me, Joe growls. I make a motion with my hand for him to sit, and he does, but his upper lip still curls into a rare snarl.

"Yes, that's me," I reply, trying to muster up some semblance of composure. Beside me, Maggie gives my hand a reassuring squeeze. I shoot her a grateful glance – she knows how to ground me.

"You're new in town?" Officer Basilier asks.

"Rebecca's the castle animal trainer—" Maggie starts to say before the Officer holds up a hand to silence her.

"She's capable of speaking for herself, I assume?" I nod. "Then tell me what you saw," Officer Basilier continues. "Why were you at the *Cafe de Flore*?" She whips out a notepad and pen, ready to scribble down every word.

"We're here to advise the Duke on the Foundation Festival," I say, choosing my words carefully. The truth is, we were hoping to have a leisurely day of taste-testing and vendor approval. *Can't hurt to make it sound more formal*, I think to myself. *If she finds out how fun our jobs are, she'll hate us even more.* "The Duke needed us to assess and evaluate the vendors. Very important job we have today."

Officer Basilier blinks at me, and it's clear she sees straight through my story.

"Interesting," Officer Basilier muses. "And how do you like working so close to the royal family?"

"Fantastic," I answer without missing a beat. "They're more down-to-earth than the tabloids make them out to be."

"Is that so?" There's a glint in her eye that tells me she's holding back.

"It's true. The Duke is a great man," I push. Beside me, Joe whimpers. Maggie stares at the sky as if there's a puzzle up there, trying to avoid making eye contact with Officer Basilier.

My cheeks flush, and I wonder if my defense of the Duke has betrayed the fact I find him quite handsome. Still, I'm too far down the road to reverse. I tell her the truth. "The Duke cares about the people here. He doesn't think Royalty should get special treatment. He's always putting the interests of the populace above his own. That's why the Foundation Festival is so important to him. It's a chance to give back and remind Monrovians about our heritage. Right, Maggie?"

"Of course," Maggie agrees. "Like Rebecca said, the Duke is a good man. He wouldn't hurt a fly."

Officer Basilier arches an eyebrow. "Such a good man that —" She checks her notes, reading off what she's written. "The crown doesn't belong on his head?" She asks, referencing the title of the article that was found in Rodrigo's hand. "A good man who had some colorful stories written about him. By none other than the dead man who was just wheeled away. Given the amount of negative coverage, one might speculate that the Duke had a motive to silence such a vocal critic."

"The Duke had nothing to do with this," I tell her, unable to keep the edge out of my voice.

"Your loyalty is touching," Officer Basilier says dryly, eyes narrowing ever so slightly. "But no one is above suspicion. The Duke, after all, believes Royalty shouldn't receive special treatment. Isn't that right?"

"It is," I tell her, ignoring the lump forming in my throat.

"You're the one who solved the murder at the castle a few weeks ago," Officer Basilier says, snapping her notebook shut and taking a step toward me. "I knew it as soon as you gave me your name. I was shocked, to be honest, that the Royal Family didn't want the local police to head up the investigation. Instead, they offered the task to their ridiculous private security—"

"Cadet Monroe," I nodded, unable to disagree with her. The Castle had transferred Cadet Monroe— who *was*, admittedly, a ridiculous person— after his most recent escapades.

When the Cadet was moved to a different post, I was thrilled to be able to avoid interacting with him. But the woman standing in front of me makes me think maybe he wasn't so bad after all. "He wasn't a real officer, that's true, so we intervened but…"

"But *I am*," Officer Basilier smiles at me. Her teeth are too pointy, flashing white against the light of the cameras. "The investigation was unprofessional, particularly given that amateurs ultimately resolved it—"

"Does she mean *us*?" Maggie whispers, deep offense in her voice.

Officer Basilier folds her arms across her chest, her eyes scanning us like a hawk— or rather, like Ace, one of our animal residents at the Castle. "There will be no civilians muddling up this investigation, regardless of whether they work for the castle or not. So, you two will do well to keep your noses out of Police business, understood? If I get even a whiff that someone from that grand house is tampering with my case..." She lets the threat hang heavily in the air before continuing, "There will be hell to pay. And charges brought."

"Understood," Maggie murmurs, her voice a mere whisper caught in the morning breeze.

"Crystal clear," I add, my heart pounding.

"Good." With a nod so brief it could've been mistaken for a twitch, Officer Basilier turns back to her work, opening up her notebook. "Now, the Cafe will be closed for the remainder of the day while we investigate the crime scene. However, we've given Jocelyn the go-ahead to keep the patio open for you to do your..." She pauses, scanning us up and down, "… very important *vendor evaluations.* The castle called the station and reiterated that it's important you have access to the outdoor space. I've decided to allow it, given that the murder was committed *inside* the shop. I see no reason why the exterior can't be made available."

"That was kind of you," Maggie says, her tone surprised.

"Not kind," Officer Basilier says, shaking her head. "Strategic." She sighs, stretching her arms wide as she checks her watch. "Per my recent phone call with the castle, I'm told your guest of honor— the Duke— will arrive any moment. Royalty is never late, even when they *are* late, isn't that the saying? Whenever a Royal arrives, they're right on time. In this case, right on time to help me with our investigation. He will be cooperative, yes? A 'good man,' as you've called him, always is."

I want to defend the Duke further, but Maggie grabs my arm and pulls me around the corner, Joe tight on my heel. As we enter *Cafe de Flore's* back patio from the street, I take a moment to glance back at Officer Basilier. She wears a satisfied expression. As an animal trainer, it's one I recognize— one I've seen on the face of a cat waiting for a bird. "The Duke's coming?" I ask Maggie, who nods.

"He had an appointment that was canceled earlier this morning," she says, suddenly worried. "I told him he should come by. He was going to join us at the end of the taste-testing. I thought it would be a fun surprise since I know you'd like to see him."

I shake my head, unable to believe the mess we've made of things. "And now… it's a trap."

CHAPTER
Four

WE STROLL into the charming patio of *Cafe de Flore*, a little oasis away from the sound of sirens on the street. Typically, it's only accessible from an exit connected to the shop itself, but Jocelyn— the cafe's owner— has opened up a heavy gate to offer access from the street. The sound of water trickling from a stone fountain blends with the murmur of voices, creating a serene atmosphere. It's like escaping to another world, and it's almost enough to make me forget about the mess going on inside the shop. The space is open and peaceful. Someone moved tables to the sides of the patio, making room for vendors' displays in anticipation of the Foundation Festival.

"Do you think they know?" I quip to Maggie, whose eyes dart around. In the middle of the patio, the vendors who've been chosen to display their goods at the Foundation Festival are clustered together in a tight circle, their expressions a mix of confusion and concern. There's Jocelyn, the owner of *Cafe de Flore*, standing by her booth adorned with books and aromatic coffees. She wears an annoyed expression, clearly bothered that she doesn't know the details about what's going on in her own cafe. Benjamin, whose youth is betrayed by his eager eyes, stands beside her— he's stepped away from his display booth for *L'animalerie Indiana Bones,* the pet supply store. Next to Benjamin is Henri, who's left the display booth for his bakery, *Le Petit Scone,* abandoned, choosing instead to join the group at the center of the patio.

The three vendors startle at our arrival, staring at us in fear.

"*C'est dangereux,*" Jocelyn says, her voice a gentle whisper. "They've shut down my store. No one has told us why! They told me to open up access from the street. They won't allow me inside my own shop! They merely said to stay outside and not to leave the patio—"

"Everyone," Maggie begins, her voice delicate as she drops the bombshell, "Rodrigo has been murdered."

A collective gasp ripples through the group. It's the kind of moment that makes you wish life came with a rewind button. The vendors take turns glancing at the display booth for Rodrigo's tabloid business. The magazines are displayed in rows, many of the editions featuring a negative story about the Duke. A light breeze whips through the patio, causing the pages of the magazines to flutter as if uttering a warning.

Beside me, Joe whines and lays down at my feet. It's as if he's taking the murder personally.

"It's okay, Joe," I tell him softly.

"Murdered?" Jocelyn's soft tone barely rises above a whisper, her hands clasping and unclasping as if wringing the tragedy from the air. "In *my* store?"

"Despite this... we'd still like to see what you've all prepared for the festival," Maggie finishes, somehow finding the right balance between respect for the dead and dedication to the event. "The Duke of Atwood will be joining us as well. I know this is shocking news, but Rodrigo was a true Monrovian who would want us to continue with an event meant to benefit the public."

The vendors glance at each other, unsure of how to proceed.

"When did you set up your booths?" I ask, interrupting the silence. A thought has occurred to me, and I pick at it, unable to leave it alone. *The vendors must have had access to the shop,* I think, realizing the implications. "I mean, what time?" I clarify.

"Everyone put their displays together last night," Jocelyn says, an edge of concern to her voice. "When we arrived this morning, the Police were already here."

"And did you personally let everyone in?"

"No—" Jocelyn stammers. "I have spare keys to the shop. All three of us had them," she motions to Benjamin and Henri. "I was planning to collect them this morning after we were finished."

"You didn't let them in from the street access?" I ask, pointing to the heavy gate that now sits open.

"I always keep that locked," Jocelyn shrugs. "Typically the trashcans sit in front of it. It was quite arduous to open this morning when the Police requested it. It was practically rusted shut!"

"So you all came in through the main store entrance?"

The group nods, confirming they all had access to the cafe — which means any one of them could have killed Rodrigo.

"What's the meaning of this questioning?" Henri sputters, his voice a deep baritone. *"Elle n'est pas d'ici,"* he adds, staring straight at Maggie.

"What does that mean?" I ask Maggie out of the corner of my mouth.

"He said you're not even from here," she mutters back, rolling her eyes. "The villagers don't like to take orders from foreigners."

"But I'm so charming!" I give Henri my best smile, but he doesn't return it. Thankfully, Maggie comes to my rescue. She claps her hands together, directing everyone's attention her way.

"We'd still love to see your displays," she motions around the space. "And the Duke will be joining us any moment now." She fans her hands in the air, motioning for the group to return to their booths. "Let's get started. *Rapidement*, before the Police change their minds. Jocelyn? Let's start with you."

Jocelyn nods, a touch of color returning to her cheeks as she leads Maggie, Joe, and me to her booth. Books are nestled amongst coffee beans and delicate cups. Whimsical twinkle lights decorate the stand, weaving in and out of fabric covers. A huge espresso machine sits at the ready, prepared to churn fresh beans into coffees on the spot. Throughout it all, intricate flowers wind their way around the booth. The display creates a tableau of literary caffeination that feels so inviting, I half-expect to find the Mad Hatter serving espressos.

"I thought it would be lovely to pair readings with themed beverages," Jocelyn explains, her voice gaining strength. She's a nervous presenter, but as she describes her ideas, her passion gives her confidence. "For example, a mystery novel reading would be accompanied by a 'cloak-and-dagger cappuccino'.'" Her eyes shine with a love so deep it could make even a non-reader consider curling up with a book. "A romance novel reading could come with a 'Love Potion' latte. We'd offer multiple readings throughout the festival, and hand out samples to guests."

"Sounds amazing," I smile, imagining the Foundation Festival filled with book lovers and the scent of freshly ground coffee. "I'd come just for the puns."

Beside me, Joe barks and wags his tail. He tries to rise on his back legs to get closer to the freshly brewed coffee, but I pull him back down to the ground.

"*Merci*, Rebecca," Jocelyn smiles at me, genuinely appreciating the compliment. "I do hope it will bring some joy, especially now that such a terrible thing has happened in my cafe

—" Her lower lip quivers and it's clear she's still reeling from the news of the murder. I can't imagine how it feels to have your own business become the scene of a crime. When I worked at the San Diego Zoo & Safari Park, the worst crime we ever saw committed on the grounds was a chimp stealing a tourist's baseball cap. I'm not sure what I would have done with a murder.

I pat her hand, attempting to reassure her. "You run a beautiful cafe. Everyone in town knows that."

Maggie jots down notes on her clipboard, and— after getting Jocelyn's signature on some participation paperwork — we move away from Jocelyn's literary oasis and onto the next booth.

When we reach the booth for *L'animalerie Indiana Bones,* the business's youthful proprietor is practically bouncing on the balls of his feet, his green eyes sparkling with enthusiasm. I take in the cornucopia of pet supplies spread before us. There are jewel-toned leashes and plush beds that look more comfortable than my own mattress, plus a smorgasbord of treats that would have any pooch doing backflips.

"I hand-beddazle the beds and leashes myself," the owner, Benjamin says, his face flushing. He can't be more than twenty-five. He's a new business owner and his nerves show it.

I hold up the harness to the sunlight, tiny blue sequins clustered together in hand-etched spirals. It's extravagant, but so is Joe.

"Let's see how it fits?" I suggest to Joe, who's been waiting patiently by my side. He perks up at the suggestion, his brown eyes pleading with hope. The promise of a cheese treat might have something to do with his sudden enthusiasm. I unbuckle his old leather collar and slip on the new harness over his fluffy gold fur. The sequins catch the light and shine like a disco ball.

"I didn't think it was possible to make Joe look any more

handsome than he already is, but you've done it," I tell Benjamin, who grins at us from behind his booth, clearly pleased that his sequined creation has found a worthy model. I remove some Monrovian cash from my bag and slide it across the table to Benjamin, who slips it into his pocket. "Keep the change," I tell him. "You earned it."

"Each pet deserves their moment of fame, just like in the movies, no?" Benjamin sweeps his hand over the display, which includes a tiny hat and whip set inspired by his hero, Indiana Jones. "I love American movies, and my favorite is Indiana Jones. Speaking of, as an American, you wouldn't happen to have met—"

"Oh no," Maggie rolls her eyes. "He asks every visitor from the United States this. Benjamin, I promise you Maggie hasn't met Harrison Ford."

"Actually, I have," I tell her. Benjamin gasps, covering his mouth. "He came to the Safari Park in San Diego once. I used to work there and I gave him a private tour. He was nice," I shrug.

Benjamin looks like he's about to pass out, but if he wants to ask more, he somehow manages to restrain himself "Um, for the festival, I'm planning a pet parade— 'The Raiders of the Lost Bark.' Each furry friend will showcase these adventure-themed accessories." He motions to a set of dog-sized leather jackets and Indiana Jones-style hats, complete with bands that go under the chin to keep them on a dog's head. "Visitors to the festival will also be invited to bring their pets and try on different outfits if they'd like. All the dogs participating in the parade will be local pets from the village."

"Adorable," I chuckle, picturing a brigade of dogs dressed as action heroes parading across the castle courtyard. I don't want to tell Benjamin so many pets in one place is a trainer's nightmare, given that dogs tend to be on their worst behavior around other dogs. I make a mental note to have plenty of treats available. "You'll have every pet owner in Monrovia lining up."

"Exactly!" He claps his hands together, clearly pleased with himself. "It's going to be *fantastique*!"

After Maggie has Benjamin fill out the required paperwork, we leave Indiana Bones behind and amble over to where Henri of *Le Petit Scone* stands stoically beside his booth. The scent of butter and sugar wafts through the air. Henri's display of pastries could rival the window of any Parisian bakery— the golden crusts of the croissants glisten beneath the afternoon sun, and the éclairs are filled with creams so lush they threaten the resolve of even the strictest dieter.

"*Bonjour*, Henri," Maggie says, her voice revealing a hint of reverence. She leans over and whispers in my ear. "Henri is a legend. His family has owned the bakery for generations." Her tone signals admiration for the age-old establishment.

"*Madame,*" Henri nods curtly, his gray mustache twitching slightly. "I suppose you're here to see how I intend to elevate the Foundation Festival."

"Please," I interject, unable to keep my gaze from the miniature towers of cream puffs. "What's on the menu?"

"Tradition," he states firmly, his accent thickening the word with importance. "You may not understand, given that you come from a country with less history. But these pastries have been the pride of Monrovia for centuries. My family recipes will be the centerpiece of the festival— time-honored flavors that remind us of our history."

"Nothing brings people together like food," I offer, earning a begrudging nod from the baker.

"Especially when it's made with honor," Henri adds, his eyes scanning his creations with a mix of pride and defensiveness. "Unlike other *newer* interests." I can't help but notice the way his eyes scan Rodrigo's booth, disdain crossing his face as he takes in the magazine covers.

"Let's hope the festival helps others appreciate it," I reply, touching my fingers to the brim of my imaginary chef's hat in salute.

"We can only hope," Henri agrees. He motions around the booth, where multiple tables have been set up as baking stations. "Each station will be set up with ingredients and tools necessary for our guests to make their own version of the classic Monrovian twisted braid pastry. I will guide them through the process, show them how to knead the dough, fold in the olives, and twist it into that iconic shape. I'll show them how to give it a golden tan in the oven."

I nod appreciatively at his plan. "Interactive. I like it."

"It's more than that," he corrects, his thick eyebrows furrowing over his silver-rimmed glasses. "It's about passing down history. It's about letting them feel, firsthand, the tradition that has been carried out in my family for generations. It's about instilling respect for time-tested methods."

"You want them to appreciate the craft behind all this deliciousness." I gesture towards the decadent spread of pastries.

He nods solemnly. "Exactly."

"Well, I'm certainly looking forward to trying my hand at it," I tell him honestly.

Henri gives a terse nod as he adjusts his tall toque hat. "A foreigner, learn to bake *our* bread?" He laughs at the idea. "We'll see about that."

I can't help but take a step back at Henri's comment. So far, my experience in Monrovia has been nothing but a warm fall into open arms. But, it suddenly occurs to me that I've spent most of my time getting to know other staff at the castle rather than the villagers. And I'm beginning to see that the villagers are a closed group who only trust their own kind. Since the day I arrived, Monrovia has felt like home—until now.

Maggie touches my arm as if she knows what I'm thinking and takes over, getting Henri to sign his paperwork. As they go through the pages together, Joe and I shuffle toward Rodrigo's empty booth. A colorful collage of sensational headlines and candid shots unravel before us. Even if I didn't like Rodrigo, I'm sad to see his legacy—a testament to the power of words, for better or worse— is at its end.

"Look at this one," Maggie says, plucking a magazine from the stand. She's finished with Henri and has decided to join me by the final booth. She pulls down a gossip magazine that features a picture of the Duke of Atwood on a yacht, shirtless. The headline reads:

Duke of Danger. Who's his latest fling?

"Can you believe people actually read this stuff?"

"Believe it? I think they live for it," I laugh, even though the pit of my stomach tightens a bit at the thought of the Duke on a yacht with a model.

Just then, a throat clearing behind us snaps our attention away from the tabloids. We whirl around to see Jack— the Duke of Atwood himself— flanked by a pair of distinguished guests. His silver hair glints in the sun, and those familiar wrinkles by his eyes deepen as he smiles my way. I've never seen a man wear wrinkles so well.

"Good afternoon, ladies," he greets us with a nod that's both regal and warm.

"Jack!" I exclaim, happy to see him. Over his shoulder, I notice Henri bristle at my use of the Duke's given name.

"Duke Atwood," Maggie nods. "You made it. The press, were they still—"

"The Police managed to make them leave for good, but only after subjecting me to quite the intense interview," Jack says, shaking his head. He stares up at the magazine covers, sadness crossing his eyes. "I wasn't Rodrigo's biggest supporter, but I'm horrified. I can't believe anyone would harm him. I'm afraid our guests are seeing us at the worst possible time." Jack motions over his shoulder at the man and woman behind him. "May I introduce Frederick, my cousin, the Duke of Highland," Jack nods at a man with piercing blue eyes and a calm demeanor, "and his sister Penultima, also my cousin, the Baroness of Highland."

"Call me Penny," the woman says. She has Jack's casual air, and if I hadn't just been told she was Royal, I'd think she was like anyone else. Her brother Frederick, on the other hand, carries himself with a Royal swagger. His chin-length hair is swept back in a greasy comb-over. He sighs as he looks around the vendors' wares.

"What a— *quaint*— festival your team has organized, cousin," he says to Jack, who glances at me with a knowing grin. He yawns, gazing at his watch. "You promised a pub in town?"

"Yes, of course," Jack says. "Maybe Maggie can show you? I'll just be a moment."

Maggie obliges, whisking Frederick and Penny out of sight. Now that I finally have a moment alone with the Duke, I feel an urgent need to tell him about Officer Basilier.

"Jack," I lean in toward the Duke, lowering my voice to a conspiratorial whisper, "Officer Basilier is sniffing around. She seems convinced you're involved in what happened to Rodrigo."

"Ah, yes, I gathered as much when I met her outside," he replies without missing a beat, the corners of his mouth twitching in amusement. "She gave me quite the inquisition. Apparently the article found in Rodrigo's hand mentioned a crown, and she's convinced it's connected to me."

"You have to be careful," I say.

"Me? Careful?" Jack smirks. "Never," he pauses, looking away for a moment, almost as if he's overcome by a sudden shyness. "But let's not allow the good officer to dampen our spirits. I'm afraid I'm forced to entertain my relatives for the time being, but I'd love assurance you haven't forgotten our dinner. I owe you and Joe, for saving my life."

My cheeks flush against my will. Beside me, Joe barks. "That's dog for 'I love cheeseburgers,'" I tell the Duke. "We're in."

The Duke exits with a smile, heading toward his cousins, but not without shooting me one last, hopeful look over his shoulder. Behind me, the tabloids in Rodrigo's booth flutter in the breeze. Who needs to read tabloids when real life keeps you on your toes?

Five

THE FLICKER of candlelight dances across polished oak as I step into the staff dining hall, a sanctuary of comfort nestled within the staff building on the castle grounds. The Duke's renovation means the staff building is a palace in its own right, located just across the shared courtyard that butts up to the castle. A symphony of clinking silverware greets me, the air rich with scents that promises a dinner to remember. I slide into my seat, the cushion a welcome relief to my weary bones after a day filled with Festival preparations.

"Ah, Rebecca, you're just in time," Chef Renauld declares, sweeping into the room like a maestro ready to unveil her masterpiece. Her wide grin is infectious, her eyes sparkling with the pride of an artist presenting her work. She's laid a feast on the table: roasted vegetables glistening with herbed oils, fresh-baked bread that steams gently when torn apart, and a roast that's so tender it practically falls off the bone at the mere suggestion of a knife.

"Chef, if heaven has a flavor, I'm pretty sure you've bottled it," I joke, earning a sly smile as the Chef takes her seat. Chef remembers every detail and doesn't forget anyone— not even Joe. He settles in at my feet with a bowl that contains the roast's organ meat. I'm not a fan of sauteed kidneys, but judging by Joe's reaction, I might just be willing to try it if Chef cooked it. My gaze wanders over the faces around the table. There's Tracey, the castle fitness expert, enjoying a green smoothie with her roast. She waves at me and I wave back, hoping she doesn't ask me to join her pilates class this weekend. Sure enough, right as I have the thought, Tracey calls out to me, "Pilates, Rebecca! Saturday. It's so good for the core."

My core has had enough, thanks, I think to myself.

Seated beside Tracey is the castle driver, Enrique, who starts up a conversation with her after offering me a wink. He's distracting her for me, and it's a gesture I appreciate.

There's a plopping sound as Maggie takes her seat beside me. She wipes a hand over her forehead. "Glad to finally sit down," she exclaims, brushing a loose blonde braid off her shoulder. "I've been running around all day, filing permits for the Foundation Festival and making last-minute adjustments to the schedule. We had to decide whether to keep Rodrigo's booth or not."

"What are you going to do?" I ask, mouth already full.

"His apprentice, Zacharia, said he can run the booth. We thought it was best to honor his memory by allowing the vendor booth to stand." Maggie leans in conspiratorially. "Have you given any thought to who might have killed Rodrigo?"

"Officer Basilier said not to snoop—" I hold my hands up in the air in mock protest. "And I happen to be very good at understanding directions."

"Which you're of course going to ignore," Maggie says, breaking open a warm piece of bread. Steam rises from the freshly baked loaf. "So, what's your leading theory?"

"Only so many people had access to *Cafe de Flore,*" I whisper, sharing the thoughts that have been brewing within me all day. "Jocelyn had a key, and she gave three other keys to Henri, Benjamin, and Rodrigo. I'd love to know if Rodrigo still had his copy when he died," I say, swirling my wine around in its glass.

"Jocelyn's always been nothing but kind," Maggie thinks aloud. "I just don't believe she would kill somebody. And Benjamin seems too busy reenacting scenes from 'Raiders of the Lost Ark' to plot a murder," she muses.

"Then there's Henri," I say, furrowing my brow. "He's as traditional as they come. He takes such pride in being Monrovian. I noticed him glancing at Rodrigo's display. I don't think he's the biggest fan of gossip magazines."

"Then he's missing out," Maggie laughs. "Nothing like a warm bubble bath and a tabloid." Maggie bites her lip, her blue eyes reflecting the flickering candles. "Do you really think one of them could be capable of such a thing? The villagers are the heart of the country. I just hate to think—"

"Who knows?" I sigh, focusing back on the plate before me. "But Officer Basilier told me not to snoop, so what's it matter anyway, right?"

"Suuure," Maggie smiles. We share a look. Deep down, we both know I'm not someone who can leave a rock unturned.

———

Later, dinner ends with the sound of cutlery scraping empty plates. Maggie leaves as soon as dessert is over, insisting she has more work to do for the Foundation Festival. When I finish my rose-flavored ice cream and pecan tart, I push my chair back, sighing heavily. My belly is round and satisfied, and at my feet, Joe snores beside his empty bowl. I give him an affectionate scratch behind his golden ears. He's lying on his back, stomach rising and falling with the sound of his breath. "Ready for a bit of a stroll?" I ask him. Joe opens one eye, looking at me like I'm an absolute lunatic. His eyebrows arch as if to say *who could walk after that meal?* "We need to burn some calories, buddy," I tell him. "It's either this or another Pilates class with Tracey."

At the mention of avoiding Pilates, Joe stands begrudgingly, his tail thumping against the floor. He probably thinks there's cheese at the end of this walk. With a chuckle, I grab his leash and we head out through the staff quarters into the cool evening air, crossing the courtyard that divides the grounds. The turrets of Monrovia Castle loom above us, giving off an aura of ancient secrets combined with modern luxury.

"Come on, Joe," I urge, as he ambles beside me with the leisurely pace of a retiree on vacation. We make our way toward the manicured gardens, passing by clusters of fragrant blooms that nod their heads as if privy to the castle's mysteries. We circle the grounds once, stopping by the rose gardens and the bird atrium, waving quickly at Alfredo the giraffe, who's asleep under a shelter I had custom-built for him. Finally, we make our way to the back of the castle where the executive office suites sit against the herb garden. As we near the edge of the garden, a sliver of light spills from an open window of the castle office. A voice drifts through the open window, and I recognize it at once, if only because it makes my stomach flip:

The Duke is in his office. And he isn't alone.

A second voice echoes into the night. And it belongs to a woman.

I know I shouldn't listen. For a moment, I consider grabbing Joe's leash and heading home. But then again, the Duke *did* leave the window open. Is it really my fault if we happen to be enjoying an evening stroll? I can't stand not knowing who the second voice belongs to, especially if it's a woman he's seeing. I'm not sure yet if our dinner plans are a date—and this might answer my question once and for all.

Rebecca, you are acting like a stalker, I think to myself. *Do not creep beneath the window of the man you have a crush on.*

Still, I bend down to give Joe a pat on the head and whisper, "Shh, buddy," before we edge closer to the window. My heart thumps in my chest as we creep around the corner, careful not to scuff my comfortable shoes against the cobblestone path. The aroma of basil and lavender wafts toward us from the herb garden as we crouch low under the window sill.

"I assure you," the Duke is saying, his voice carrying the crisp note of formality touched with a hint of weariness. "I have nothing to hide. You're welcome to scrutinize my every move; you'll find no fault."

The reply comes sharp and unyielding, like the snap of a whip. "Your cooperation is appreciated, your Grace, but platitudes won't sway investigative procedure. You are now officially a suspect in the murder of Rodrigo Lopéz. I'd advise against any travel plans."

Suddenly, I recognize the woman's voice. It's Officer Basilier.

He's invited her to the castle to answer more questions? I think, unable to believe the Duke would engage in such a dumb idea. Then again, the more I think about it, the more it makes sense. Jack believes in equity. He believes in transparency. He's honorable. So honorable that he might just accidentally send himself straight to prison.

My mouth goes dry like one of Chef Renauld's biscotti left out overnight. Joe lets out a low whine, sensing my sudden alertness, and I place a calming hand on his back. I hold a flat hand in the air— our training signal for quiet— and Joe crouches low toward the ground, burying his face in his paws.

"Understood, Officer," the Duke replies, his tone betraying a flicker of indignation. "Again, I must reiterate. I have answered all your questions— I will cooperate in every aspect of the investigation. I expect to be treated just as everyone else. But I must ask…"

"Yes?"

"Do you truly think your suspicions of me *are* treating me like everyone else? Would you be so intent on assigning presumed guilt to me if I were not Royal?"

"You are a suspect based on evidence found at the scene of the crime, possible motivation, and means," Officer Basilier insists. "You yourself have admitted you resented the stories presented by Rodrigo in the tabloids—"

"And yet I selected him to be a vendor at the Foundation Festival!" The Duke exclaims.

"Perhaps in order to have access to him and more easily rid yourself of his stories once and for all. He was found holding a story with the title *'The Crown Doesn't Belong on His Head.'* If I didn't consider you my main suspect, I wouldn't be performing my duties. I'm sure that's something you understand, isn't it? Duty."

The Duke sighs, and I peek over the window sill, catching a glimpse of his dismayed expression. He shakes his head. "It seems, for all my attempts at fairness, life remains a game of power."

"Meaning?"

"Meaning," the Duke continues. "We all have our blind spots, Officer Basilier. I only hope yours won't be my undoing, costing Rodrigo the justice he deserves in the process. I ask you for a fair investigation not as your Duke, but as a citizen of Atwood. That is all."

There's a silence that hangs heavy in the air as the Duke's words ricochet across the night. Officer Basilier clears her throat. I peek over the windowsill again, watching as she closes her notebook and stands, squaring her shoulders defiantly. "Stay within the country, *your grace,*" she says, emphasizing the title of respect with particular venom. "We'll be in touch."

I duck beneath the windowsill as the sound of a door slamming rocks the space. Together, Joe and I retreat from our eavesdropping spot, running across the grass into the herb garden, our breath coming out in a fog against the night. My legs burn as I pick up the pace, forcing us to cross the courtyard as quickly as possible. We run from the scene, and Joe huffs in response, probably wondering if this escapade will ever lead to a warm bed and a bedtime snack.

Finally, we reach the staff quarters and push open the double doors, making our way back to my unit. When we reach my apartment, I flip the lights on, chasing away the shadows. Joe flops onto his plush bed with a sigh of relief. I want to sit next to him. The thought of what the Duke might be facing is so awful I want to curl into a ball and worry about nothing except training animals.

Instead, I head toward the hall closet and open it, retrieving my trusty corkboard from within. I remove the accompanying stand and set it up in the hallway like an artist with an easel. The corkboard fits on top with ease. Next, I grab some paper from my printer and hand-write the names of our potential suspects. *Jocelyn. Benjamin. Henri.*

I pin their names to the board, each accompanied by a string of information encompassing everything I know so far. The stores they own. Their connection to Rodrigo. Every little detail goes up on the board. On another piece of paper, I write the words that we found clutched in Rodrigo's hand— the title of the article he never got to publish.

"The Crown Doesn't Belong on His Head."

"Jocelyn, Henri, Benjamin..." I mutter to myself, sticking pins into the board with more determination than a seamstress on a deadline. "One of you knows who killed Rodrigo, and I'm going to find out who."

Joe watches me with half-lidded eyes, entirely unconcerned with the gravity of the situation, and possibly still hoping for cheese.

When the job is done, I brew a cup of tea and sink into the familiar embrace of my favorite armchair— the one with the slightly worn fabric on the arms where Joe has claimed his spot more times than I can count. He seems to read my mind, and with a contented groan that speaks volumes about his love for routine, he jumps onto the armchair and curls up beside me, his weight too heavy on my lap but somehow still comforting.

The day's chaos settles into a hushed stillness, broken only by the soft clinking of the teaspoon against my teacup as I stir in a dollop of honey. The steam from the chamomile infusion carries a promise of calm, and I take a moment to breathe it in, feeling the warmth seep through the porcelain and into my palms. Outside, Monrovia's coastal breeze whispers secrets to the ancient stones of the Castle.

"Okay, Rebecca," I whisper to myself, allowing the friendly tone of my own voice to steady my racing thoughts. "It's time to put on your detective hat. Metaphorically speaking, of course. Hats mess with my hair."

Taking a sip of tea, I let it ground me before turning my mind to the task at hand. I don't want to prove the Duke's innocence just because I've taken a liking to him, although it's true— I have. I want to prove his innocence because I know how it feels to be seen as an outsider. I'm new to Monrovia, and the villagers see me as a stranger. The Duke may be a Royal, but in his own way, he's also someone who's seen as "other." It must get lonely. And when it comes to clearing his name, he's clueless.

Jack's going to get himself sent to prison before I even get the chance to go out on a first date with him.

"Looks like it's up to us, buddy," I say. Joe wags his tail at me, telling me he approves of this unexpected turn of events. We'll have to be quiet about our efforts and avoid Officer Basilier. But together, I know we can crack the case.

And just like that... We've signed on for an adventure.

CHAPTER
Six

CRISPY FRENCH TOAST with crème fraîche melts in my mouth. Even though I'm focused on my breakfast, I can't help but chuckle at Maggie's puzzled expression. We're enjoying another one of Chef Renauld's incredible breakfasts in the staff dining hall, and despite the delicious food, Maggie is horrified at my recounting of last night's events. "The Duke invited Officer Basilier to the castle? Is he daft?" she exclaims, disbelief crossing her face as a wayward piece of toast drops from her fork.

"Self-preservation isn't his strong suit," I reply, glancing down at Joe, who is happily gobbling up poached eggs from his bowl near my feet. "I'm starting to think our Duke takes the idea of fairness and equity a bit too far. If I were Royal and a suspect in a murder investigation, you can bet I'd use my privilege to save my behind. I wouldn't do well in prison. I get upset when the elevator doors take too long to open. Can't imagine getting stuck in a tiny box."

Maggie lets out a sigh. "So, what's the plan, Sherlock?" she teases, her eyes sparkling with mischief. She knows exactly what I'm up to.

"Elementary, my dear Watson," I say, winking over the rim

of my coffee cup. "We're going to crack this case wide open. And I need your eagle eyes and rosy outlook."

"Really?" Her voice lifts in excitement. "You want my help again?"

"Of course! Who else would keep me from saying stupid things, and laugh with me when I inevitably do?" I grin, leaning back in my chair. Maggie's become a friend, and I can't imagine looking for trouble without her.

"That's good because I need a break from all the phone calls and work emails." She leans forward, whispering guiltily, "I was kind of sad when we solved the last murder. Like, I was happy my name was cleared, but I also missed having something to investigate, you know what I mean?"

"Uhm, Maggie. If we hadn't solved that murder, you'd be in *jail* right now."

"I know, I know," she says, waving a hand at me as if ending up in jail is besides the point. "I'm just saying— it was fun being detectives!"

"Well I'm glad you liked it, because it looks like we get to do it again," I say. "First stop, *Cafe de Flore*. We'll have a little chat with Jocelyn and get more information about the cafe."

"Oooh, and maybe grab one of her Lavender Lattes for the road?" Maggie suggests, hopeful.

"Only if you promise not to spill on the evidence," I tease.

———

Atwood Village is a sleepy place this morning. The sun kisses the tops of the buildings as Maggie, Joe, and I stroll through the winding cobblestone streets, his golden coat shimmering. His tail sways like a lazy metronome, keeping time with our pace.

"Remember, we have to keep our sleuthing to ourselves. Otherwise, Officer Basilier will find some reason to come after me using the law, " I say. Beside me, Maggie takes a bite of her pastry. She grabbed one of Chef Renauld's breakfast offerings to go, and now, she's eating it like it's the last one she'll ever have. "If Officer Basilier could put me in jail tomorrow, I think she'd do it," I continue.

"There's no pastries in prison," Maggie says, chewing loudly. "We can't allow you to end up in a pastry-less jail cell. Mums the word."

As we approach *Cafe de Flore*, the air simmers with the scent of roasted coffee beans and the sweet perfume of the flowers that grow up the side of the cafe's exterior wall. The Police are gone— all of the crime scene tape from yesterday has been removed. *Cafe de Flore* has been restored to its usual beauty. It's as if nothing grim ever touched this quaint spot. I push the door open, a familiar jingle announcing our arrival.

"*Bonjour*, Jocelyn!" I call out, but no one answers. We peer around the empty cafe. The lights are on, but there's no sign of anybody home.

"Maybe she stepped out?" Maggie suggests. Suddenly, Joe puts his nose to the ground, walking across the cafe toward a door to the side of the coffee bar. The door sits ajar, issuing an invitation I can't resist. Joe whines at us, urging us to join him. We follow Joe, pulling the door open to find a messy office space. Jocelyn stands in the center of the chaos, arranging a bouquet of Petunias in a vase. She startles when we open the door.

"*Mon dieu!*" She exclaims. "You frightened me." She puts a hand to her chest, exhaling with relief. "My apologies. I've been on edge since—"

She doesn't finish her sentence, but she doesn't have to. Maggie nods with understanding. We noticed a change in the Village during our walk to the shop. It feels less safe since Rodrigo's murder. Atwood is usually a place where people leave their doors unlocked, but since his death, a subtle cloud has hung over the town.

"I'm so sorry," I say, shaking my head. "We didn't see anyone at the register."

"It's so slow this time of day," Jocelyn agrees. "I stepped into my office to try a new floral arrangement for the tables. Can I help you two? A latte or—"

"Actually," I admit, sitting at a chair across from her. "I wanted to talk to you about the murder. I'm friends with the Duke and the lead officer thinks he had something to do with it when we all know he would never—"

"The Duke?!" Jocelyn exclaims. "*Non.* The man is a Saint. Not a murderer." She continues arranging her flowers. Maybe she's just engaged in the task, but part of me wonders if she's trying to avoid my questions by keeping her hands busy.

"That's why we wanted to know… Did you notice anything… *different,* on the morning Rodrigo was killed?"

She pauses over a petunia, its delicate petals straining under her grip. "Nothing at all," she replies, her tone as smooth as the foam on her lattes. "It was just an ordinary day until… well, everything happened. I had come in the night before to set up my booth, like everyone else. I stayed late, but as I was leaving, Benjamin came in after me. Henri was still there when I left. I assume the two of them disappeared by morning. When I came in to open the cafe I was sent directly to the patio. Rodrigo was already dead, and the Police had been called. It was quite a shock, seeing the authorities outside my little store." She shivers at the memory.

"And the keys?" I prod gently. "Did all the vendors return them the next day?"

"Everyone but Rodrigo," she confirms, her smile faltering for a split second before it returns, unwavering. "So tragic." She turns to fuss over the bouquet again, her back to us as she adds flowers to the opposite side. "I did not ask the Police if they found the key on Rodrigo's body because, well, I assumed they had bigger problems to attend to. It seemed in poor taste, *oui?*"

I nod, trying to look casual when I'm hanging on her every word. A bell rings from the cafe's main lobby. Another customer has arrived, and by the sound of their throat-clearing, they're eager for service. "Excuse me," Jocelyn says, delighted to leave us. "I'll just be right back—" She exits, heading for the counter.

"Looks like someone's been doing more than flower arranging in here," Maggie whispers, eyeing the scattered papers and half-open drawers. She's right. In stark contrast to the book-laden, flower-dotted cafe, Jocelyn's office is a mess. Piles of papers sit on the desk, and the room is strewn with cardboard boxes. I lift the lid on a box labeled "receipts." Inside, hundreds of slips of paper float around in no particular order.

"Her poor tax accountant," I say sadly. "He must be a tortured soul to put up with this…"

Joe makes his way around the desk, a sniffling sound coming from his nose as he investigates the space. He stops at a drawer, frozen. As a trainer, I recognize the dog's body posture as one not to be ignored. It's a stance that says he's found something. He whines at the drawer and I move toward it, pulling it open to see what's within.

Joe's nose doesn't disappoint; he's led me straight to the dirt. Tucked away in the drawer are old, dog-eared editions of Rodrigo's gossip rag. I leaf through them, ignoring the cover stories and stopping at earmarked pages. On each one, there's a scathing review of *Cafe De Flore.* They span multiple years, going back as far as a decade. Gripping snippets such as "Culinary Calamity" and "Espresso Exasperation" are among the kinder phrases. The meaner ones? Well, I won't repeat those in good company.

"Look at these," I motion to Maggie, who joins me, reading the articles over my shoulder. "It seems Rodrigo was just as hard on Jocelyn as he was on the Duke."

"Wow," Maggie breathes, her voice laced with disbelief.

"Who doesn't love *Cafe de Flore*? I hope Jocelyn didn't take these reviews too seriously."

"If she did, it would explain why Rodrigo's dead," I tell her, nodding somberly. "Maybe he pushed her too far," I mutter, thumbing through the pages. It's not just the harshness of the words that strikes me—it's the betrayal that Jocelyn, who pours her heart into this place, must have felt when she read them. Rodrigo's reviews evaluate the cafe through a lens of cynicism. He saw her floral arrangements as trite. Her decor as too cutesy. The cafe itself as too whimsical. There's no denying it— the reviews read like a personal attack.

I'm about to pull another magazine from the pile when the sound of approaching footsteps makes me snap the drawer shut. Jocelyn's coming back. I tuck the magazines into the small of my back, hidden under my jacket in the waistband of my pants.

"Today will be a busy one," Jocelyn says as she re-enters, her kind smile intact. "Can I interest you two in a drink? A lavender latte, perhaps?"

"I can't say no to that," Maggie chimes in, and honestly, neither can I. We thank her and follow her out to the counter, leaving the office—and the mess within—behind us.

"Thanks, Jocelyn," I say, meaning it. Whether she's guilty or not, she's been nothing but kind. "For the chat and the coffee. We love your cafe, you know. *Cafe de Flore* was the first place Maggie showed me when I moved to Atwood. It's one of my favorite spots, here. It makes me feel at home."

Jocelyn blushes as she makes our lattes, looking genuinely touched by what I've said.

"Thank you," she tells me, making foam art on the top of our drinks. "I take pride in my business. It's like a piece of me. If it makes you feel at home, I'm doing something right."

She slides the drinks across the counter. Maggie and I exchange glances as we exit the cafe, Joe leading the way like he's got somewhere important to be.

"Did you hear what she said about the cafe?" Maggie asks, a worried expression furrowing her brow. "Jocelyn's so sweet. I just can't picture her as a murderer."

"She'd be the world's nicest murderer," I agree, thinking about how Jocelyn has been kind to me even though I'm a foreigner. I've noticed that other villagers tend to look at me sideways, as the American intruder with a big dog. But Jocelyn always makes me feel at home.

"But the cafe means everything to her and if Rodrigo threatened it in his reviews—"

"Maybe she threatened *him*," I say, nodding.

"But that doesn't explain the page he had in his hand," Maggie says. "*The Crown Doesn't Belong on His Head*."

"Maybe the lead was unrelated to the murder," I say, thinking out loud. "Perhaps it was just an unhappy accident that Rodrigo happened to have a royal report in his hand. Either way, Rodrigo really had a knack for making friends, huh?" I quip, trying to keep the mood light despite the fact one of the nicest people we know is now our top suspect. "The Royals... Jocelyn... Rodrigo gave plenty of people a reason to hate him. Not great at making friends, is he?"

"Besties all around," Maggie agrees, dryly using the American word for best friends I've taught her. But even as we laugh, there's a weight to our steps—a shared understanding that we're getting closer to something. Something dangerous, and maybe even deadly.

CHAPTER
Seven

THE NEXT MORNING, I wake up to slivers of light seeping through the curtains, their gentle rays making me stir awake. The mattress groans as I roll over, discovering Joe sprawled out beside me, snoring softly like a furry old man. His golden coat is a messy tangle— he needs a bath, but the task will have to wait. We have too much to do today. Maggie warned me last night that she'll be busy making arrangements for the Foundation Festival all day long, which leaves the investigating to Joe and me. We'll visit the castle animals first and tend to their needs, then conduct a training session with Ace the red-tailed hawk. But after that, we're free to snoop around.

With a determined stretch, I slip out of bed and nudge Joe awake. "Adventure awaits," I tell him. Joe doesn't budge. Apparently solving a murder isn't enough to get him out of bed. "Also… *breakfast*," I add, emphasizing one of his favorite words. The clarification seems to do the trick. He sits up at once, his enormous head of crazy hair making him look like Einstein.

"Come on, you big lump," I chuckle, ruffling the tuft of

tendrils adorning his forehead. "Let's see what Alfredo the Giraffe is up to."

Joe's ears perk up at the mention of our tall, pasta-loving friend. Alfredo might be a giraffe, but he appreciates fine dining as much as anyone. Over the past few weeks, Alfredo and Joe have bonded despite being different species. I suspect their connection is over a shared love of food. Joe rolls onto his paws with a groan, the promise of seeing one of his pals motivation enough to get him moving.

For Joe's morning walk, we take our usual path around Castle Monrovia's grounds, the dew-kissed grass soft under my feet. The air is crisp with the scent of the nearby ocean mingling with the castle's manicured gardens. As we walk, I can't shove aside my thoughts about Rodrigo's murder. The title of the article we found in Rodrigo's hand flashes before my eyes:

"The Crown Doesn't Belong on His Head."

It's possible whoever killed Rodrigo stole the rest of the article, which means they didn't want the story to get out. It occurs to me that Rodrigo's apprentice— Zacharia— might know something about the lead. Maggie said he's still operating the newsstand in the village. After our chores are done, Joe and I will make sure the newsstand is our first stop.

We finish our walk back to the staff quarters, swinging by the dining hall to see what Chef Renauld has cooked up. On alternating work days, she puts out a grab-and-go continental breakfast instead of a sit-down meal. Today, there's silver catering trays of egg-and-cheese breakfast sandwiches. I grab one for me and one for Joe, who eats his in a single bite. A tea station lingers near the exit, and I pour myself a hot cup of English Breakfast into a disposable to-go cup. Then, we're on our way.

When we reach the animal courtyard, Alfredo the giraffe is already awake. He stands beneath a tree, his long, giraffe neck towering over us, looking down at me with expectation. "Morning, Alfredo," I greet the giraffe, who seems to nod in response. "Pasta for breakfast, as per your unusual tastes." I used to try to force Alfredo to eat more appropriate meals, but in the past few weeks, we've reached a compromise and managed to meet each other halfway.

Joe greets his friend with a nudge to the leg. Alfredo returns the gesture by stomping his enormous hoof on the ground. I'm sure it's his way of telling Joe he's pleased to see him.

I reach into my backpack and pull out a previously frozen batch of white-sauce Alfredo pasta. Alfredo's eyes widen in anticipation, his long tongue peeking out to taste the air. Earlier this morning, I removed the pasta from the freezer in my apartment, which is full of similar plastic containers. I asked Chef Renauld to make batches in advance that I can allow to thaw before my visit to the giraffe, and they've taken over my freezer. My walk with Joe was just enough time to get the sauce to melt. I can't help but laugh as I toss a handful of noodles high into the air, Alfredo catching them mid-fall with an eager chomp.

Joe watches with envy, but I remind him with a pat, "You've already had your breakfast, buddy." He seems to whine a little, but perks up when he's able to grab a noodle Alfredo dropped just for him. Eventually, he resigns himself to lying in a nearby patch of sunlight.

When the job with Alfredo is done, I move on to the brand new bird atrium, which the Duke ordered be built at my suggestion. It's three times the size of the barn the birds were kept in previously and open to the air, secured with mesh wiring. Inside, two bald eagles roost. A series of finches take flight. Joe and I feed and water them all, stopping at our red-tailed hawk friend. "Alright, Ace, your turn," I say. The hawk eyes me from his perch, his gaze sharp and intelligent. He hops onto my arm like a practiced expert, his claws gripping the leather glove I've put on for protection.

I carry him out to the courtyard, and we go through our training session with precision, Ace swooping and diving with a grace that makes me feel like I'm up there with him. "Good boy, Ace. You're more reliable than some humans I know," I tease the bird, earning a dignified ruffle of feathers.

We put Ace away, and— on our way out— stop to feed the alpacas and zebras that free-roam the courtyard, their soft coats a pattern of colors against the green backdrop of the grounds. We leave them more bushels of hay and steel containers of feed, and—finally— we're ready to put our detective hats back on.

"Okay, Joe," I announce, "Let's chat with Rodrigo's apprentice."

Joe wags his tail as we walk toward the bridge that leads to the village.

A short stroll later and we're ambling down Atwood's cobblestone streets, my boots clicking rhythmically against the stone. We weave through the town, passing by tables laden with colorful fruits and vegetables outside the green-grocer's, the vibrant displays a stark contrast to the pastel hues of the surrounding buildings. Above us, the banners for the upcoming Foundation Festival flutter like hopeful pennants in the breeze. Villagers bustle about their business, their energy a low hum beneath the clanging of the cafe's cups and the sound of a musician playing violin on the street. We pass by the central square's bubbling fountain, stopping at the statue of Monrosha, the founder of Monrovia. She's regal in her posture, and I can't help but think how glad I am to be in a country with such an interesting history. It's nice to know that Monrovia was founded by a female leader who cared about people more than anything.

"Smells like Henri's been busy," I murmur, glancing at Joe,

whose nose twitches with interest. We're only a block away from Henri's bakery, *Le Petit Scone*, and the scent of his pastries calls to me. "But first, work before pleasure."

We make our way to the next block over, where Rodrigo's newsstand still stands, unchanged since his death. The stand is made of sturdy wood, each shelf overflowing with stacks of colorful, glossy magazines begging to be picked up and flipped through. The covers are adorned with bold font and salacious headlines, tempting readers with scandalous gossip and juicy celebrity secrets. The latest one hits home:

*"GOSSIP REPORTER FOUND DEAD! IS THE
CROWN TO BLAME?"*

I pick it up and thumb through the story, shaking my head.

"Too soon?" A voice asks behind me. I turn, discovering a thin man in his late twenties. He's lanky and clean-cut— Rodrigo's opposite in every way.

"Rodrigo might think it's soon," I shrug. "But you knew him better. You're his apprentice?" I ask to confirm.

"Zacharia," the young man says, reaching out to shake my hand. I shift the magazine I'm holding into my opposite arm to accept the gesture.

"Seems like you're moving on with… grace," I observe.

He throws his hands in the air defensively. "Look, I'm just doing what Rodrigo would have wanted. He taught me you never leave a scoop behind, even if it's wrong. Even if it hurts. He never thought *he'd* be the scoop, but still— if it were me lying in that coffee shop he'd do the same thing. And he'd expect nothing less of me now." Zacharia puffs out his chest as if he's proud of himself.

"Sounds like Rodrigo taught you well," I say, dropping the magazine back into the display. "I was the one who discovered him that morning."

"That was you?" Zacharia says, his eyes wide. "Maggie told me she was with someone else who works at the castle. I'm sorry, that must have been—" His eyes water a little, and I can see there is genuine care there for Rodrigo, even if care won't stop a scoop. "…Awful."

"It was," I answer. "It's stayed with me. That's why I wanted to ask you about Rodrigo. About the article that was found with him. The headline was all that was left and it said": *The crown doesn't belong on his head.* Do you have any idea what that means?"

"Rodrigo was always secretive about his leads," Zacharia sighs, pushing back his dark hair with a hand. "But he did tell me he had a beat that could shake Monrovia's high society. He seemed excited about it. Almost like he wanted to tell me but couldn't. He kept it top secret, even from me."

"Did he meet with someone about it?" I ask. Zacharia nods. "Any clue who?"

Zacharia leans in conspiratorially. "He met someone at a casino. Wouldn't tell me who. You know, protecting his source until the story ran. All I know is he hung out at the bar, went to play Blackjack, and came back the next morning looking like he'd won the lotto."

"Rodrigo didn't keep digital files, did he?" I ask, hoping there might be a way to retrieve the remainder of the ripped story. If Rodrigo kept files on his computer, maybe Zacharia can help me access them.

"Digital? No way. Rodrigo was old school— he used a typewriter to get his leads on the page. He said no hacker could break into his accounts and get to his stories that way. He kept everything offline and hardcopy. He'd type on that typewriter for hours. Didn't go near a computer until it was time to format the magazine and the story was ready for press. He took the typed stories straight in to the printer, who formatted everything for the next day's press."

"Seems like a lot of work," I agree, unable to believe

Rodrigo didn't keep digital copies. "You're *sure* he never used a computer or—"

"He was old school," Zacharia confirms.

"No kidding," I say, shivering as I remember Rodrigo's body on the floor of *Cafe de Flore*. The ripped page in his hand might have meant he was on his way to put the story in for publishing. Whoever killed him might have stopped the beat mere hours before its release. "Thanks, Zacharia. You've been very helpful."

"Of course," he nods, pointing at the magazines behind him. "Hey, and if you hear any juicy gossip at the castle, you know where to bring it."

I laugh, "Sure thing."

He leans in, arching an eyebrow. "I mean it though," he nods gravely. "Rodrigo left me the magazine stand and I want to do right by him. You know, keep the stories flowing. You could be a great source because you work at the castle! Stories about the Duke sell out every time. I can pay you. Think about it."

"Okay," I lie, knowing that I will never— not once— give Zacharia information about the Duke of Atwood. I can't imagine betraying him.

After waving goodbye, Joe and I leave the gossip stand behind. We head down the street, thinking about what we've learned. *Zacharia had a lot to gain by Rodrigo's death,* I can't help but think. And he sure seems enthusiastic about running the newsstand in his absence. Is it possible Zacharia killed Rodrigo to take over the stand?

I'm lost in thought, but Joe snaps me out of it. He's been patient with me, but I notice his gaze lingering on a passerby holding a cheese croissant. "We could use one of those, couldn't we bud?"

We amble towards *Le Petit Scone*, Henri's quaint patisserie. It's a charming little bakery, its exterior adorned with large windows that showcase delicious pastries and treats. A bell clangs as we push the door open, revealing a cozy interior decorated with warm colors, vintage wallpaper, and sparkling marble countertops so clean you could eat off them. The air is cloyingly sweet, filled with the aroma of freshly baked pastries and bread. Hints of vanilla, cinnamon, and butter color the shop.

"Come on, Joe," I say, nudging him up to the bar. "Let's grab some of Henri's famous pastries to go."

We bend down to the pastry case looking for cheese, but it's a twisted braid of bread that catches my eye, savory black olives winking through its doughy folds. I remember Henri describing the cake as a Monrovian classic at our vendor day.

"Two of those, please," I tell the girl behind the counter, pointing at the braided breads. "And… is Henri here today?" I try to sound casual as I ask the question, but the truth is, I'm hoping to talk to Henri about Rodrigo's murder.

"*Non,*" the girl shakes her head. "He stepped away."

She passes me the braided bread and I try not to let my disappointment show as I pass her cash across the pastry case. Questioning Henri will have to wait for another day, but I was hoping to catch him now. Still, a single bite of the pastry makes my bad mood fade— it's a savory delight. The bread's crispy, golden-brown crust gives way to a soft, fluffy interior. The salty, briny flavors from the plump olives woven throughout the dough melt in my mouth, and a quick look at Joe tells me he feels the same. He gobbles down the bite I've passed him, getting crumbs in his mane before looking at me for more.

We leave *Le Petit Scone,* a cool breeze sending fallen leaves skittering across the cobblestones. Joe and I make our way down the winding alley toward the central courtyard fountain and pass the statue of Monrosha. I'm about to lead us back to the castle when a shadow falls over us.

"Miss Orange!" A voice calls out behind me.

We turn, discovering Officer Basilier. She's in her uniform, looking cropped and prim. Her lips are pressed into a hard line.

"Officer Basilier," I reply, lifting a hand in greeting, clutching the almost-empty bag of pastries a little tighter. Joe lets out a low growl before sitting by my side. "We were just getting second breakfast," I say, holding out the bag of pastries and attempting to look innocent.

"That's interesting," she replies, her skepticism apparent. "Because Zacharia at the newsstand just informed me you were asking questions."

"Guess I should've expected the gossip writer can't keep a secret," I mutter, shaking my head. "It isn't a crime to be curious, is it?"

"A reminder, Miss Orange," Officer Basilier steps toward us, her shoulders square. "Leave the investigating to the professionals. Curiosity may not be a crime, but interfering with an investigation certainly is. I would hate to see you occupying one of our jail cells."

With that, she turns on her heel, leaving Joe and me alone in the courtyard.

CHAPTER
Eight

A CHORUS of scents swirls around me as Chef Renauld's latest culinary creation is placed before us on the table. Savory herbs intermingle with delicate notes of a tangy sauce. My stomach rumbles as I prepare to taste the Chef's latest masterpiece— lobster and caviar risotto with a champagne cream sauce. I can practically hear angels singing in the background, but that turns out to be Maggie, who exclaims, "I can't believe Rodrigo wrote everything with a typewriter!"

"Right?" I respond, nodding vigorously. I've just filled her in on my investigation from earlier in the day, and she seems as baffled by the typewriter revelation as I am.

Under our feet— Joe, who's become Chef Renauld's biggest fan— is already face-first in his specially prepared doggy dish. At the other end of the table, Tracey— the fitness expert— sips a purple smoothie alongside her risotto. She's deep in conversation with Monique, who's still in her maid's uniform. Beside them, Enrique sets his driver's hat on the table, looking at the risotto with all the eagerness I feel. The entire staff is here tonight. No one is willing to miss Chef's best dinner of the week.

"Anyway," Maggie continues, lowering her voice conspiratorially, "I accidentally did some investigating of my own." She pauses to take a bite of the risotto, savoring it for a moment before continuing, mouth full. "I was working with the Duke to plan the Foundation Festival today, and he mentioned that Officer Basilier has it on good authority that the note in Rodrigo's hand was something really juicy. Apparently, she interviewed the woman who owns the printing shop, and she said he called her the night before saying he had the biggest story of the year. He told her he needed it to go to print first thing in the morning. He promised the printer he was heading her way right after the vendor show was finished. Of course, he never got the chance given he was—"

"— Murdered?" I answer through a bite of my meal. She nods.

"Exactly. So Officer Basilier called and told the Duke all this, only so that he legally understands why he's going to be detained at some point. Dealing with Royalty is a legal minefield, so she called the Duke as a courtesy to tell him to get his affairs in order. She'll be publicly announcing him as an official suspect any day now."

"She *can't!*" I exclaim so loudly that other staff members at the table look up at me in surprise. I clear my throat, lowering my voice to a near-whisper. "I mean, he's innocent."

"It's terrible too because he's got so much on his plate right now. I *know* he wants to go to dinner with you—" She winks at me, and I feel my cheeks flush against my will.

"I figured he'd forgotten…"

"Of course not," Maggie waves a hand. "He's desperate to have a night of fun. He's been swamped, what with the Foundation Festival and his relatives in town— we met them, remember, Frederick and Penny?"

I nod, recalling Frederick's arrogant presentation and Penny's seemingly sweet demeanor. The siblings couldn't be more different.

"They're a tough pair of guests," Maggie sighs, shaking

her head. "Frederick is impossible to please. No pillow is soft enough for him. No activity is interesting enough. The maids have been so busy balancing all his requests. Penny puts up with it all. It's a shame he's the heir to the Highland title. Penny would be better— she's the nicest person. But he gets the Royal title because he was born a couple of years before her. That's why he's the Duke of Highland, and she's just a Baroness."

"That's too bad," I say solemnly, thinking of the statue of Monrosha in the Atwood Village Courtyard. Something about Penny reminds me of the country's founder. When I met Penny, she had the same regal air, combined with a warmth in her expression. "Penny would be better than Frederick at holding a Royal title."

"I agree," Maggie nods, taking another bite of her food. "But anyway… the Duke's been busy with his guests, and then there's a mess of a situation with the seaports near Highland where all our imports come through by ship—" She waves a hand in the air. "It's all keeping him on his toes. But I know you'll get an invitation to a dinner with him soon." She grins at me as if she knows something about a secret I'm not in on.

Our meal passes quickly, and by the time dessert arrives, the warmth of the staff dining hall wraps around us like a cozy blanket. We dig into the evening's final offering— exquisite peach tarts with cream. The delicate crust crumbles in my mouth, surrounding juicy peaches that make me feel like I'm biting into summer.

After dinner, Joe and I make our way back to my apartment, guided by the soft glow of the hallway sconces that decorate the corridors of the newly renovated staff quarters. I've always admired that the Duke— who could've saved a pretty penny by choosing cheaper fixtures— chose instead to make the staff quarters just as beautiful as the castle itself. We reach the front door to my space, and— as soon as we enter

— Joe flops down onto his favorite rug with a contented groan.

"Someone's ready for bed," I chuckle, scratching him behind the ears before freezing in place. There's a crunching sound beneath my feet. I lift up my shoe, revealing a crisp, white envelope that's been slid under my door. The royal seal decorates the envelope's surface, and my name is written on the front in formal calligraphy.

My heart skips a beat— the envelope must be from the Duke.

There's a ripping sound as I tear it open and begin to read:

> *Dear Miss Rebecca Orange,*
> *The Duke of Atwood formally requests your presence at a private dinner tomorrow evening in the Royal Dining Hall of Monrovia Castle. Formal attire is encouraged. If your driver requires specific accommodations, please have them contact the attendant below. We eagerly await your esteemed presence.*

"Driver?" I say out loud, laughing to Joe, who looks at me with wondering eyes. "Maybe they've got the wrong Rebecca. This invitation is for dignitaries."

I flip the invitation over, discovering a hand-written note from Jack on the opposite side. It reads, simply:

> *You saved my life. At least let me feed you. P.S. Joe too? – J*

I can't help but smile. Every now and then, my life in Monrovia feels like a fairytale (minus the murders, of course).

"Wow, Joe," I say, looking down at my faithful companion. "Looks like we're moving up in the world." Joe wags his tail in response, seemingly as excited about the prospect of a fancy dinner as I am.

"Better start looking for something to wear," I muse, already mulling over the limited wardrobe I brought with me when we moved here. There's nothing formal in my closet, and this sounds like a fancy occasion. But one thing's for sure – if Jack wants to thank me for saving his life in person, I'm not going to miss it. Even if I have to attend in my tennis shoes.

CHAPTER
Nine

THE NEXT MORNING, crisp air nips at my cheeks as Joe and I amble along the castle's perimeter, our breathing heavy as we take our morning walk. The castle courtyard is a beautiful sight this early, and I love exploring the grounds before anyone else is awake. It's a medley of lush greens and vibrant florals, with neatly trimmed hedges and ivy-covered walls that run the length between the staff quarters and the castle itself. The sun's soft light weaves through the openings in the stones, hinting at a dew-dripped morning that will melt into sunshine by the late afternoon. In front of a vegetable patch, Douglas, the Groundskeeper, tends to a patch of cucumbers. He offers us a hearty wave, pushing his hat back over his head. The scent of freshly cut grass mingles with blooming flowers as Joe and I loop around the space in a circle that leads to the section of the grounds where the animals reside.

We stop to feed and water the zebras, and briefly check on the hay bails for the rest of the hooved creatures that roam the grounds. After visiting Alfredo the giraffe in his enclosure— where he's sleeping soundly— we walk toward the staff quarters to change into nicer clothes. But before we can reach the building, Joe's ears pin back to his head. He freezes in place.

"You hear something buddy?" I ask, listening. A pair of voices emanates from over the hedge, where the herb garden lies. And not just any voices: a pair of *angry* voices.

Joe and I look at each other, then creep closer. I peer through the hedge. In the herb garden, the Duke's family visitors— Frederick and Penny— are standing across from each other, both of them looking outraged. Penny has her arms crossed, her cheeks reddened. Frederick has his finger in her face, his eyes wide.

"And who are *you* to tell me— the heir to our family title — how I am to run my life?" He shouts at her.

Penny's eyes water. She looks as if she might cry. Even from this distance, I can see the concern etched into her delicate features. "Your gambling will be the end of you," she says, her voice shaking. "It's unbecoming, especially for someone of your standing."

"Stick to your books and botanicals, Penny," Frederick hisses back, just loud enough for me to catch. "Keep that sharp nose out of my affairs."

"You have people who are *depending* on you," Penny cries, pointing into the distance at an imaginary crowd. "Subjects. Citizens. The people of our town, of Highland, depend on *you* to ensure their fortunes! You could make a real difference if you tried. You could create employment opportunities. You could fix the issues with the deliveries from sea—"

"The imports are fine," Frederick waves the issue away.

"You could do so much to improve the lives of our constituents," Penny pleads, the earnestness in her voice truly moving. "I had hoped vacationing here would give you new perspective. But you're too busy spending your days at the Blackjack table."

"You know nothing," Frederick says. He spits on the ground, then turns on his heel, leaving a rattled Penny alone in the herb garden. I want to comfort her, but I'm afraid revealing my presence will only make the situation worse.

Instead, I shrink away from the hedge, trying not to rustle the branches and give away our presence.

"Let's leave the aristocrats to their secrets," I mutter to Joe, who gives a lazy wag of his tail as if to say 'your drama is my drama.' With a final glance at the siblings, I steer us back onto the path to the staff quarters, unnoticed by all.

After a quick shower and a change of clothes, Joe and I meet Maggie by the castle gates. We've all agreed to walk to the Village Atwood together. Maggie has some items she needs to pick up for the Foundation Festival, and— under the guise of running errands— we plan to investigate Rodrigo's murder.

The three of us set off down the cobblestone path, and in no time at all, we reach the village of Atwood. Pastel buildings unfurl before us like a pastel quilt. Joe trudges beside me, his golden coat gleaming. His pace lags as he pretends he's not utterly thrilled by the promise of new scents and canine companions.

"Looks like someone could use a double shot of espresso," I tease, nudging Joe with my foot.

"Or maybe just a cookie," Maggie suggests, pointing ahead to where *L'animalerie Indiana Bones* sits nestled between a florist and a dressmaker. Its window stands out against the others on the row— in the display, cardboard cutouts of dogs are dressed in Indiana Jones costumes.

"Benjamin's shrine to Hollywood," I say as we push open the door, greeted by the chorus of barks and the comforting smell of kibble and leather.

Inside, the walls are plastered with movie posters, from dusty deserts to jungles teeming with danger—all starring the intrepid Indiana Jones. It's part pet store, part Hollywood homage, and visiting the space feels like going on an expedition. Even the dogs milling about seem to have caught the adventurous spirit. There's a small corgi in the corner who looks ready to fight with a sturdy bulldog. He growls, and his teeth gleam. The bulldog's owner bends down to give them each a cookie and the tension passes.

"Did I mention Joe has a bad habit in pet stores?" I whisper to Maggie, just as Joe, ever the opportunist, spies an open bin of cookies. He ambles over, glances back at me with what can only be described as a look of mischievous triumph, and snatches a biscuit with the stealth of a seasoned cat burglar.

"He's a thief," Maggie laughs.

"Joe, you rascal," I chide, though there's no bite to my words. "At least try to pretend you're not a complete hooligan."

Maggie giggles. "He's just embracing the shop's spirit—Indiana Bones and the Temple of Snacks."

"I'll pay for it later," I promise, as Joe, content with his pilfered treasure, settles onto the cool tile floor, the very picture of innocence.

We wander through the aisles, examining rows of different harnesses and leashes. I notice a special section dedicated to Benjamin's hand-bedazzled creations, and I'm pleased that I had Joe wear his sparkly blue number today.

"Benjamin," Maggie waves at the shop owner, who's stocking a nearby shelf with bird food. He waves at her, and his smile grows a little too big when he sees her. For a moment, I wonder if he's interested in Maggie as more than a friend.

If that's the case, I hope he's not our murderer, I think to myself.

"You guys need something for the castle animals?" Benjamin asks, dusting his hands off on his apron. "Rebecca, that palette of zebra feed you ordered won't ship for a few more days. Everything has been delayed because of the port situation in Highland. I just checked the delivery time last night—"

"No worries," I tell him, waving the idea away. "Actually,

um, we stopped by because—" I struggle to address our real reason for visiting.

"We wanted to talk to you about Rodrigo," Maggie said, lacking all subtlety. "Rebecca's investigating the case, and anything you know could really help us." She leans up against the aisle of animal feed, batting her eyelashes at him. Benjamin seems to melt in her presence.

"Oh sure, anything I can do to help," he says, nodding. "I didn't spend a lot of time around Rodrigo though..." he starts, shaking his head. "He had a way of making things... difficult."

"Difficult how?" I ask.

"His stand..." Benjamin gestures vaguely toward the wide windows, where a view of the exterior street unfolds. The gossip magazine stand is visible across the cobblestone road. "It's close to the shop, which he hates. I put out signage in front and he claimed it blocked pedestrians from easily accessing his newsstand, which is nonsense, of course. He just didn't like that my Indiana Jones displays distracted from his gossip magazines. But who *wouldn't* choose a fun store with animals and movies over glad rags?"

"True," Maggie nods her head, agreeing. "What you've done in here is cute. I'd pick it over a smelly newsstand any day."

"Exactly," Benjamin agrees. "But Rodrigo didn't like that our shop was getting more attention. He blew up one day at my Dad about the signs being out." Benjamin looks at me to clarify. "My Dad co-owns the store with me," he explains. "Anyway, he was shouting at us on the street. Ever since then, I've stayed away from Rodrigo. But I swear I'd never wish him harm. Competition is one thing. What happened to him..." Benjamin shudders.

I nod, filing away every inflection, every frown line etched into his youthful face. There's genuine disgust, there. He doesn't strike me as a killer.

"Oh no," Benjamin stares at the dog-washing station, his

face blanching. "Poppy the Pitbull is here and she has a meltdown at the water-sprayer every time. Do you mind if I just…?" Benjamin excuses himself, leaving Maggie and me alone in the aisle.

"Doesn't seem like a killer, does he?" Maggie asks.

"If he is, he's one with a crush on *you*," I say, and despite herself, Maggie's cheeks flush.

———

Later, Maggie, Joe, and I make our way to *Le Petit Scone*, our final stop in town. We're hoping to pick up pastries, and maybe also interview Henri.

"Remember," Maggie whispers to me as we push open the front door. "Don't approach Henri directly. He'll be offended if he thinks you're calling him a murderer."

"Wouldn't anyone?" I ask, rolling my eyes.

"Yes, but when Henri gets offended, plates get broken," Maggie says, laughing as we enter the quaint store that's a picture of tradition. The warm embrace of freshly baked goods swirls around us, sugar and butter clinging to the air. By my feet, Joe audibly sighs. There's nothing he loves more than bread, except, maybe— cheese.

A quick glance behind the counter tells me we're in luck today. Henri, the stalwart guardian of Monrovian pastry, is elbows deep in flour, his grey mustache flecked with white shrapnel like a general in battle.

"*Bonjour*, Henri," Maggie calls out, waving at him.

"Ah," he grunts, barely looking up. "Miss Maggie. Rebecca. What brings you here today?"

"Besides your world-famous scones?" I quip. Henri doesn't laugh.

"Those will be at the Foundation Festival," he says, nodding toward a mountain of pastries. "A special creation, just for the event. But I suppose I can offer you a preview?"

"Thank you," Maggie agrees. She taps her foot on the ground as Henri generously passes us two pastries. I take a bite. Raspberry jam explodes in my mouth. Henri may be gruff, but he's generous.

"Henri, these are amazing," Maggie says, chewing gently. Her eyes scan my face— she's trying to find a way to bring up Rodrigo without alarming Henri.

"I can't wait for the festival," I say, treading carefully. "It's just such a shame Rodrigo won't be there."

"Yes," Maggie nods, catching my drift. "I keep thinking about it and it makes me so sad."

Henri looks up from kneading his dough, offering a *harrumph*. "*Oui*," he says, nodding. "His death is tragic. But his absence at the festival? It may be for the best. He did not belong there in the first place."

"Why do you say that?" I ask, taking a step forward.

"You would not understand as you are not from Monrovia," Henri says, looking at me skeptically. "But here we value culture. Tradition. An old way of doing things. His reporting on the Royals was improper. Shameful. I was shocked the Duke invited him to be one of the chosen vendors. It casts a shadow on our principles."

I'm about to ask Henri more about his dislike for Rodrigo's reporting, but a cashier on the other end of the bar waves him over and we lose his interest. Begrudgingly, Maggie, Joe, and I make our way out of the bakery, beginning the long walk back toward the castle.

"Henri is such a traditionalist," Maggie sighs, linking her elbow with mine as we navigate the cobblestone path leading away from Henri's bakery and toward the heart of Atwood Village. "But I don't think he would've killed Rodrigo over it."

"Maybe not," I say, mulling over everything we learned today.

"Earth to Rebecca," Maggie teases, using one of the American phrases I taught her. She waves a hand in front of my face. "You're lost in thought. Could it be about your date with the Duke tonight?"

My stomach turns. I'd forgotten all about my plans with Jack during the sleuthing.

"*Is* it a date?" I say, suddenly worried. "I mean, did he *tell* you that it was?"

"It's a dinner," Maggie shrugs, a knowing look in her eyes. "That's all." She pauses. "So, have you decided what you're wearing?"

"I think I'll just show up as *me*," I answer, thinking through my wardrobe of t-shirts and jeans. "I have one dress I brought, which means it's the choice. Joe has it easier because he's got that great natural coat."

Maggie pats my arm. She can tell I'm nervous. "Rebecca, you train exotic animals for a living. You wrangle zebras before breakfast and teach alpacas to dance the tango. You've got this."

"Sure, but do zebras care if my dress matches my shoes?" I quip, trying to mask my jitters with humor.

"Jack won't care either," Maggie assures me. "Just be your-self. Remember, it's just dinner, not an audience with the Queen."

"Right... unless he brings his aunt, who literally *is* the Queen," I add with faux horror, earning another round of laughter.

CHAPTER

Ten

JUST KEEP BREATHING, *Rebecca,* I think to myself. My chest rises as I obey my own orders and take a deep breath. Joe and I are standing outside the doors to the Castle's royal dining hall. The dress I'm wearing is a short black one— it's nothing fancy, but it fits me like a dream. I didn't have any heels, so I've paired it with my sneakers. Beside me, Joe wears a bow tie around his neck, compliments of Benjamin.

"Ready, bud?" I say. He seems to nod at me, and we push open the double doors.

Stepping into the royal dining hall of Castle Monrovia is like wandering into one of those museum paintings you're afraid to get too close to, just in case you sneeze and ruin centuries of history. The chandeliers are dripping with crystals that scatter light across the room. Ornate tapestries adorn the walls, depicting scenes of Monrovian lore, their threads telling tales of pirates at sea and a monarchy-led kingdom.

"Wow," I murmur, freezing in place. This is a room so beautiful that I feel like I'll get in trouble if I touch something. Joe, on the other hand, seems convinced this room is like any other. He saunters forward, unimpressed by the grandeur, more interested in visiting his favorite person.

The Duke of Atwood— Jack— is already seated at the center of a long table that could easily fit the population of a small village. It's decked out in fine china and gleaming silverware. Two servants stand at attention at the perimeter of the room, ready to cater to our every whim – or so it seems.

"Hey there, little man," Jack ruffles the top of Joe's golden head before standing to greet me. "Rebecca," he says, reaching out to take my hand. He leads me to the table with that charming half-smile of his, pulling out a chair for me. "A spot for you, and of course, a spot for Joe." The Duke gestures to a plush pillow beside my seat, complete with a miniature dining setup that somehow manages to be both regal and ridiculous.

"You didn't," I laugh, whistling at Joe, who leaps at once onto his pillow throne. "This is way too much for us."

"You two deserve it," Jack says, pushing my chair in as I sit down. In the past, dates have tried the gesture, but it's always ended awkwardly. With Jack, though, it's effortless. He's been raised to drip with charm. "You saved my life, and you've made the castle animals feel quite at home. It's the least I can do."

Jack sits beside me, and I feel relieved. The table is enormous, and I was worried he'd sit at the other end, leaving me alone in a sea of mahogany. Jack seems to catch my gaze. "The table is huge," he agrees. "It's been in this room since the late 1800s. I would have chosen a more intimate venue, as this is usually reserved for dignitaries, but—" he pauses, searching for words. "I wanted you to have everything special. To *know* that you deserve the best." He scans my face looking for approval, and when he doesn't immediately find it, seems to backtrack. "Maybe we should have done a simple coffee? Or perhaps, a place in the village. I didn't know what you would prefer and Maggie thought the best of the best was a safe bet—"

Is he… nervous? I think to myself. I reach out and touch his hand.

"This is amazing," I say. "I'm so happy to be here." I want to add *with you*, but I bite the words back. The Duke relaxes a little, relieved.

The food arrives, carried in on silver platters that are lifted to reveal a feast fit for, well— a Royal and his company. The scent of roasted meats and fresh herbs fills the air, and my stomach growls in approval.

"Apologies for the delay arranging this dinner," Jack says once we've begun to eat. His fork clinks against his plate as he slices through what looks like the tenderest cut of beef I've ever laid eyes on. "The unexpected arrival of Frederick and Penny has kept me quite busy."

"Sounds like you have a full house," I comment, savoring a bite of something green and buttery. I do my best not to drop any crumbs— the evening is so formal, I'm afraid to make a mess. Joe, meanwhile, scarfs down a morsel of chicken from his special dish, spreading gravy everywhere.

"They didn't tell me they were coming for a visit. It's quite unusual actually. Royal protocol is that guests request an audience months in advance. But Frederick just— showed up." He shrugs, leaning in conspiratorially. "Frederick, much like me, has always eschewed the typical way of doing things. The difference is, I spend my time promoting a more egalitarian, modern monarchy, and Frederick, I'm afraid, gambles and drinks."

"We all have different ways of coping," I laugh.

The Duke smirks at me. "True. All this to say, I've wanted to see you but it's been quite difficult to shake my cousins. They've been glued to my side. It's also kept me from solving the trouble with our imports—"

"Maggie mentioned something about that," I say, taking another bite.

"It's terrible," the Duke sighs. "It's a problem with the

ports in Highland. All of our imports for Atwood come through the coastal town. But the ships arrive empty! Thieves have been intercepting deliveries even when we change the schedule. It's impacting imports significantly."

"Pirates?" I ask, aghast.

Jack laughs. "Modern pirates, yes. I was hoping Frederick could help offer some perspective given his position at Highland, but he's been— less than useful."

"Sounds almost like they know when the shipments are arriving," I muse aloud, tapping my table with my fingers. "Have you asked around to see if there's a leak from the department that knows the schedule?"

"That would be quite impossible because—" the Duke freezes mid-bite as if something I've said has registered with him. He sets down his fork, looking me up and down. "Actually," he sighs, nodding at me. "You've given me a lead to look into. One I'd prefer not to chase, but your clever mind has found it all the same." He smiles at me, those wrinkles by the corners of his eyes making me melt. "If you hadn't become an animal trainer, perhaps detective would have been your alternate life."

"Being a trainer is actually similar," I tell him, smiling. "Animals are puzzles to solve. You have to watch their behavior and understand what it means, just like people."

Jack's eyes meet mine, and for a moment, his easy-going demeanor falters, revealing a hint of the weight he carries on his shoulders.

"Rebecca, I'm truly grateful for what you did last time," he says, his voice almost a whisper. "Your knack for unraveling mysteries saved my life. This new mystery, though? I fear it might not turn out as favorably for me. Officer Basilier is... Well, she's relentless. She believes in justice without exception, and I'm afraid she may soon announce me as a suspect."

"Because you wanted to be treated like everyone else?" I

ask, my brow furrowing in concern. "It's a noble cause, to live by the same laws by which you govern."

"Exactly," he nods solemnly. "But that nobility might come at a steep price. I'm only telling you this because, I—" he reaches out for me, placing a hand on my knee. "I don't want you to get involved. I know you love a puzzle, but Officer Basilier has it out for me. I would feel—" Jack looks for the word, "— *destroyed* if my station in life complicated things for you. I must ask you not to investigate Rodrigo's death. It isn't safe."

I look down at the floor. There's no way to tell the Duke I'm already investigating. And I won't make him a promise I can't keep. Instead, I look back up at him, smiling a little.

"Jack," I say, shaking my head. "You were made for this, you know that?"

"Made for what?" he asks, alarmed.

"Being Royal. You're as valiant as Monrosha, giving up her last piece of bread for the people," I say, thinking about the statue of her that stands in the village square. "You were *meant* to be a Duke because you can uphold a form of leadership that comes from a place of service. It's—" The words feel right, echoing the bravery I've seen in him since we met. "It's beautiful."

"Maggie's been teaching you our history, I see?"

I shrug. "I may have also stopped by the library a few times."

Jack leans in, and I'm suddenly aware of how close he is. "When I met you and Joe on that plane, I could tell— you had Monrovian spirit. You've proven me right at every turn." He smirks. "And I like to be right."

For a moment, I feel as if we're the only two people in the world. But then a dessert tray lands in front of me, and a white-gloved server leaves two pieces of divine cake in front of us. We separate, both of us feeling as if we've been caught.

"Being Royal means rarely being alone, I'm afraid," Jack whispers to me. But he can't erase the smile in his eyes.

———

Later, when dinner is finished, Jack insists on what he calls *escorting me home.* We stroll together toward the staff building, and I resist the urge to hold his hand.

Treading across the cool stones of the path that winds through the courtyard, I can't help but feel a bit like Cinderella after the ball— not that I'm expecting my shoes to disappear or my coach to turn back into a pumpkin at any moment. The moon hangs heavy above Monrovia Castle, bathing everything in silvery light, and there's a slight chill in the air that makes me grateful for the warmth of Jack's coat over my shoulders.

"Beautiful night, isn't it?" Jack's voice is soft beside me, his presence comforting in the vast expanse of the open space.

"Stunning," I agree, glancing up at the stars peeking through the night sky. "Walking across this courtyard is like a fairytale."

"One with a dashing Duke?" he teases, a twinkle in his eye that suggests he's thoroughly enjoying the role of my escort.

"Obviously," I chuckle, nudging him playfully with my shoulder. "Though, in a fairytale, the Duke usually has a bit less trouble with the law."

"Ah, well," he sighs, the humor briefly fading from his expression. "Every hero has his trials, I suppose."

We reach the staff quarters and Jack stops outside the doors. Joe pants by my feet, exhausted from a long day. He looks at the Duke and tilts his head as if he's inviting him in.

"This is where I leave you," Jack says. I remove his jacket and pass it back to him, sad to return it. "And, Rebecca," the Duke continues, "I know you are a bold woman who will do whatever you must but please—" his eyes darken. "—

Consider what I've asked. Stay away from this mystery. Officer Basilier is not one to be trifled with."

"I can promise to *consider* it," I smile, knowing full-well my consideration will lead to a decision to continue.

Jack laughs, shaking his head. "I suppose that's all I can ask. Perhaps you'll allow me to enjoy your company again. If not at something so formal. Maybe a simple—" He pauses, unsure of what to suggest.

"Coffee," I agree. "Coffee is perfect."

"Coffee it will be," he smiles. He takes my hand and kisses the back of it, pressing his lips into my skin, allowing them to linger just a second too long.

"Goodnight, Rebecca," he says. And with that, he heads across the courtyard back to the castle, his form disappearing into the night.

I look down at Joe, who wags his tail at me.

"Who needs glass slippers anyway, right buddy? Sneakers seem to work just as well."

CHAPTER
Eleven

LIGHTBULB MOMENTS DON'T USUALLY strike at the crack of dawn, but here I am, eyes popping open before the sun has fully risen. Joe's snores— a rumbling purr—fill the room as I shuffle out of bed. The idea that woke me up seems to have been in the back of my mind all night, and now it's fully formed, begging me to act on it.

"Joe," I murmur, watching one gold-furred ear twitch in response. "The Duke said his cousins visited him without warning. Don't you think that's strange for Royals?"

Joe tilts his head in agreement.

"We've got a mystery to unravel today, bud." With some encouragement, I manage to get Joe out of bed. I throw on jeans and my favorite sneakers, hoping I can catch Maggie at the dining hall. She's always up earlier than me, but today we might bump into her.

The dining hall smells like fresh croissants and coffee— enough to lure even the most devoted sleeper from their bed. Grabbing a plate, I pile on a miniature feast, casting a glance at Joe. He had one of his dog pâtés this morning, but I slip him half a croissant anyway.

"Rebecca, you're up early," Maggie chirps from behind us, her voice bright. "How was last night with the Du—"

"I'll have to tell you later! There's something too important. I couldn't sleep, and was hoping to run into *you*," I confess, stirring cream into my coffee. "My brain's been doing cartwheels." I take a sip of my coffee, letting the warmth wake me up. "You know our unexpected guests, Frederick and Penny? Jack told me last night they showed up unannounced."

"And?" Maggie asks, confused.

"And something doesn't add up. I'm not sure if it's related to Rodrigo's murder, but I want to do a little digging— see what they're *really* doing here."

Maggie's eyes widen, a mix of surprise and concern flooding her irises. "What's the idea?"

"I want to offer them an animal tour—the private kind. Today." I grin, feeling a little like a detective in a cozy mystery novel—one who swaps magnifying glasses for leashes. "It'll be 'educational' for them and enlightening for us. Jack said they've been glued to his side anyway, so this offers the added bonus of giving him some space. Can you set it up?"

"I'm on it," Maggie says, setting down her croissant and typing quickly into her cell phone. "I'll arrange it for this afternoon."

———

Hours later, and Maggie's been true to her word. I wait outside the animal courtyard— Joe standing at attention beside me— when we're greeted by the sight of Frederick and Penny ambling over from the castle. Frederick wears a beige blazer, his hair slicked to the side, gaze disinterested. Penny, however, looks every bit the eager tourist in her floral dress and bright smile.

"Good morning!" I beam, clapping my hands together.

"Ready for an exclusive tour of Monrovia Castle's finest non-human residents?"

Penny's face lights up like she's just won a golden ticket to the zoo. Frederick, on the other hand, manages a grunt that could either be agreement or an indigestion warning.

"First stop," I say, leading them into the bird atrium, "is our very own feathered escape artist, Ace the Hawk."

The bird atrium is a symphony of chirps and tweets, sunlight filtering through the glass ceiling and casting a kaleidoscope of light on the lush greenery. Ace, perched majestically atop his stand, eyes us with a disinterest that rivals Frederick's.

"Isn't he amazing?" I gush, hoping my enthusiasm is contagious.

"Absolutely stunning," Penny agrees, her gaze locked on Ace's sharp profile.

Frederick checks his watch. "How long does this tour last?"

"*Frederick*—" Penny protests, clearly embarrassed.

"I'm not the one who wanted to see the animals," Frederick says, rolling his eyes.

"It's not too long," I assure him. "Only as long as your curiosity can bear," I quip, offering him a smile that I hope doesn't look too much like a smirk.

We move on, leaving the aviary behind as we step outside into the rolling green grounds. The zebras graze peacefully, their stripes a stark contrast against the vivid grass. "Zebras have stripes as unique as human fingerprints, with no two zebras having the same stripe pattern," I tell them, enjoying Penny's look of awe as she pets one of the exotic animals. "They're the only animal with black and white stripes from nose to tail, and their true coloring is actually *all* black. This is because their skin is black and the white stripes are formed by lack of pigmentation in certain areas. They have excellent eyesight, with a field of vision of 300 degrees."

"Look at how they chew," Penny whispers, utterly charmed.

"Yep, they're nature's lawnmowers," I deadpan, earning a soft chuckle from her.

Our next—and unexpectedly final—stop is Alfredo the giraffe, whose lanky neck peeks out from his enclosure like a periscope. Joe barks at the sight of his favorite friend, then offers a perfect "sit" pose in the hopes of getting a treat. I toss him one for good behavior.

"Would you like to feed some Alfredo to… *Alfredo*?" I ask, reaching into my bag and pulling out one of the thawed pasta dishes before offering it to Penny.

She nods enthusiastically, stepping forward to offer the pasta, which Alfredo accepts with a delicate grace that belies his size.

"Isn't he adorable?" Penny coos, clearly smitten. Alfredo's tongue wraps around the plastic dish.

"Adorable," I echo, watching the gentle giant munch contentedly.

Then, the universe decides to add its punchline. As Alfredo shifts, something else drops—a pile of giraffe-sized poop. The mess lands squarely in the worst possible spot—on Frederick's polished shoe.

"Disgusting creature!" Frederick recoils, his face contorting into a scowl.

"Animals will be animals," I say, the corners of my mouth twitching.

"I've had just about enough for today," Frederick says, shaking off his soiled shoe with a grimace. "I'll be at the pub, Penultima. Don't wait around for me." With that, he disappears, leaving us behind in his angry wake.

As he storms off, I turn back to Penny, who looks mortified. "I apologize," she says, shaking her head.

"Don't worry about it," I assure her. "Alfredo didn't mean anything by it—it's just another day at the castle for us."

"Thank you, Rebecca," Penny sighs, relief flooding her features.

Pasta strands dangle from Alfredo's mouth like some sort of bizarre spaghetti waterfall, and even though Frederick stormed off with a scowl that could curdle milk, I can't help but chuckle at the giraffe. Penny giggles, too.

"This tour has been the highlight of the trip," she says, nodding at me. "I can't thank you enough. My brother's been so difficult lately. This was a nice escape."

"Really?" I prompt, seizing the opportunity for a little digging. "Is everything okay?"

"I don't know," she shrugs. "It was all his idea to visit the Duke out of the blue. Thought it would be a 'jolly good fun trip,' or something like that." She rolls her eyes. "I was hoping the vacation would give him a new perspective given the opportunity to see how hard our cousin works for the people, but it appears not to have made any impression."

"Has he... always been so impulsive?"

"Frederick? Oh, heavens no." Penny sighs, tucking a loose strand of hair behind her ear. "Lately, he's just been... different. Moodier. He's been haunting the pub more than his own home, forgetting appointments, misplacing things..." Her voice trails off as she watches a zebra march to the edge of the giraffe enclosure, perhaps hoping for some pasta.

"Being a Royal must be difficult," I say. "I can imagine he feels pressure."

"More than you know," Penny continues, frowning slightly. "But it's more than that. He's gambling a lot these days. More than usual. It's like he's trying to outrun something, or maybe himself. The town of Highland could use his attention instead," she murmurs, almost to herself. "If I were in charge there's so much I would do. But—" she pauses, remembering that I'm there.

"But what?" I ask.

"Birth order," she says. "The firstborn takes the Royal title unless they do something terribly illegal that disqualifies them from the role. That's the way Monrovian law is written. So I dedicate myself to supporting Frederick and try to help him become the best leader he can be— for our people. That's what Monrosha would have done."

"I recently learned about her legend," I tell Penny. "I think you're honoring her memory by being selfless."

"I only wish my brother could do the same," Penny says. "He's more interested in the next poker game than his subjects' well-being. His life has been difficult, given that our parents died when we were quite young. But he wasn't always like this. It's just— after the tragedy— he never managed to find his way. Only the poker table makes him happy."

I nod sympathetically, imagining a once-dedicated man losing himself to the allure of chance and risk. The story is painting itself in shades of gray, and I can't help but wonder if Frederick's sudden visit and his recent behavior are pieces of a larger, more complicated puzzle.

"This vacation isn't over yet. Maybe this trip really *will* do him some good before you leave," I offer, meeting her gaze. "A change of scenery can work wonders."

"Perhaps," Penny replies with a small, hopeful smile. "Or maybe it'll just give him new places to forget things."

We share a quiet moment of understanding before I open up the gate, ushering Joe through and waiting for Penny to follow. "Come on, there's still plenty more to see. And who knows, maybe the fresh Monrovian air will jog something loose in that brother of yours."

"Or at least keep his shoes clean," Penny quips.

"Exactly," I agree, leading the way. "Now, let's go make friends with a zebra or two. They're excellent listeners."

I lead Penny toward the zebra enclosure, allowing her to mix and mingle with the animals. But although my body is present with her, my mind is somewhere else. I can't stop thinking about Frederick's strange behavior. Could the article in Rodrigo's hand have been referring to Frederick when it spoke of a crown?

The idea appeals, but still, the pieces don't make sense. Frederick isn't even *from* the Village of Atwood, so there's no way his path would have crossed with Rodrigo's. Not to mention, he still has no clear motivation to murder.

As my last case showed me— just because I don't like someone, doesn't mean they're a killer. In fact, it can be the people you least suspect who turn out to be criminals.

CHAPTER
Twelve

I'M in the dining hall— mid-bite of an egg fried over-easy, the kind that leaves gooey evidence all over your lap if you're not careful— when Maggie practically bounces in her seat. "Guess what I found out?" she chirps, sitting down next to me at the staff dining table, her braids swaying with excitement.

"Tell me," I say, brushing dripping yolk from my mouth with my napkin. At my feet, Joe's already finished his breakfast, and now, he's eyeing mine.

"Okay, so, after our interview with Henri the other day, I did some digging —" She pauses for dramatic effect, sipping the cup of tea she poured herself before joining us. "Before Rodrigo's murder, Henri sent an email to the castle claiming Rodrigo shouldn't have been selected as a vendor for the Foundation Festival."

"Really?" I set down my cup, a little too hard perhaps—tea sloshes onto the saucer. "What does our cranky baker have against Rodrigo being part of the Foundation Festival?"

Maggie's eyes widen, animated. "Oh, it was quite the read! Henri's disapproval wasn't just a passing comment; it was a full-on diatribe. He thinks Rodrigo's involvement tarnishes the tradition of the festival. He says being selected as a vendor is a prestige honor that should have gone to a different business in the village. And he was very vocal about Rodrigo bringing shame to Monrovia. That's a strong sentiment to put in an email. Henri must have been angry."

"He'd have to be, to put it in writing." My eyebrows hitch up a notch. I lean back, the chair creaking under my weight as the gears in my head start turning. Could Henri's traditionalism and his love for Monrovia have driven him to kill Rodrigo?

"It's time for another visit to *Le Petit Scone*," I say, thinking out loud. "Maybe I can get Henri to talk." I stand up, dropping my fork on my plate. "Do you want to join us?" I ask Maggie.

"I can't," she says, face falling. "I have to help Douglas get the Castle grounds ready for the festival. He's pulling up all the weeds and freshening the flower beds with new annuals. But good luck! Tell me everything when you get back."

———

After finishing our duties to the castle animals, Joe and I step out into the crisp morning air, headed for the Village Atwood. Joe seems to share my mood, his gold fur catching the first rays of sunlight as he trots beside me, tongue lolling in that carefree way dogs have mastered. The cobblestones click beneath my sneakers, each turn through the village streets revealing another quaint view straight out of a storybook.

"Ready for some sleuthing, Joe?" I ask, though I know he's more interested in sniffing every lamppost than in my detective ambitions. He barks in response, which I'll take as a yes. We weave past the pastel-colored shopfronts, a soft chatter from al fresco diners seasoning the morning bustle.

The bell above the door tinkles as I push into *Le Petit Scone*, and a wave of warmth greets us—a stark contrast to the brisk outside. The bakery is abuzz with the sounds of sifting flour and clinking trays. Henri is in his element, loading an array of golden-brown deliciousness into boxes stamped with the Foundation Festival's logo.

"*Bonjour*, Henri," I venture, offering a smile to cut through his brusqueness.

"Ms. Orange," he replies without looking up, his nod as curt as his greeting. Joe, untroubled by social cues, makes a beeline for a tray of twisted braid cakes.

"Easy there, big guy," I chuckle, reeling Joe back before he starts a culinary catastrophe. "We're here on business, remember?"

Henri finally lifts his gaze, his eyes narrow slits of suspicion. I stand my ground, unfazed. After all, it takes more than a grumpy baker to intimidate Rebecca Orange, animal trainer extraordinaire—and now, amateur sleuth.

"Seems like you've got your hands full with the festival prep," I comment casually, leaning against the counter with all the ease of a regular.

"*Oui*," he grunts, sealing the last box with a definitive thud. His mustache twitches, and I wonder if it's an involuntary reaction to my presence or just crumbs seeking escape.

"Looks delicious," I add, letting my gaze wander over the pastries, though my appetite is for answers, not almond croissants. "I'm sure it'll be a hit at the festival."

He nods again, the briefest lift of his grey brows acknowledging the compliment.

"Henri," I begin, my voice soft but firm, "I heard about your email to the Castle. The email you sent asking that Rodrigo be removed as a festival vendor."

"*Ma lettre?* What of it?"" His hands pause mid-pack, bread loaves momentarily forgotten.

"You seemed quite passionate about Rodrigo not being part of the festival."

"Passion has nothing to do with it," Henri retorts, his

French accent thickening with emotion. "It is about respect—respect for tradition, for Monrovia!"

"Ah, tradition," I muse, a small smile playing on my lips. "The sacred guardian of pastries and festivals alike, *n'est-ce pas*?"

"*Oui*," he agrees reluctantly, and I swear I see the corner of his mouth twitch. Deep down, I believe Henri *wants* to like me, and he would— if I weren't a foreigner. "Rodrigo was a..." He hesitates, searching for a polite term, then gives up with a shrug. "… A stain on our country's honor. A gossip columnist does not belong in the most prestigious event of our year. He reflects the worst of us, not the best" Henri pauses, realization crossing his face. "My goodness, are you— do you suspect that I would have harmed him?"

"I'm not saying that," I shake my head. "I'm just trying to get to the bottom of things. They're blaming the Duke, you know."

Henri gasps. "The Duke would do no such thing." He puffs out his chest. "And neither would I. Everything I do comes from pride in being Monrovian. Monrovia is a civilized, peaceful country. We are not murderers."

The sound of a throat clearing echoes behind me. I whirl around, finding Officer Basilier, a dark look crossing her eyes. "Officer," I say, my heart skipping in my chest.

"Rebecca," she says my name as if it's a curse word. "I see you're keeping *busy*."

"Busy with scones, that's me!" I say, suddenly struck by the urge to run. I turn back to Henri and order two scones for Joe and me. He slides them across the counter with haste and accepts my cash at once, both of us hoping to end the interaction as quickly as possible. "Bye, Henri, keep the change!" I call over my shoulder as Joe and I make a run for it.

The bell clangs as we exit the store and I think we may have gotten away, but I'm only a few steps down the road when Officer Basilier's voice calls out behind me:

"Rebecca. Stop."

I freeze in my tracks and turn to face her, sweat dripping down the inside of my arm. Beside me, Joe whines, hiding behind my legs. Officer Basilier approaches us with a slow, steady gate, her hand on the waistband of her pants.

"Miss Orange," she begins, her voice sharpened to a point. "Your interest in this investigation is becoming quite the village spectacle. Care to enlighten me on your intentions?"

I turn, offering her my most disarming smile. "Oh, you know, the usual: scones, tea, and a side of absolutely no sleuthing whatsoever."

Her eyes narrow, unamused. "This isn't a game. And if you're not careful, you might just find yourself in the middle of the next headline. Especially with the surprise that's brewing for our dear Duke." She tilts her head ever so slightly, as if daring me to ask more.

"Surprises can be nice," I quip, though my mind races. "You don't mean a birthday party, do you? Because I'm terrible at baking cakes."

Before she can retort, Joe makes a coughing sound, wagging his tail with feigned innocence. But it's too late; she's already spotted the pastry wrapper— an unfortunate souvenir from *Le Petit Scone*— drifting onto the pavement from his mouth.

"Ah, and littering, too," she says, plucking the evidence from the ground with a swift motion. Her pen clicks as she scribbles out a ticket with mechanical precision. "Merits a ticket. You'll owe a fine." She rips off a piece of paper, passing it to me.

"Of course," I reply, accepting the ticket with an apologetic nod.

Basilier thrusts the slip into my hand, her gaze unfaltering. "Miss Orange. Stay out of this case, or the next time I see you, I'll be arresting you for interfering with an investigation.

Monrovia takes pride in its laws, and we don't need outsiders interfering. Understand?"

"Understood," I assure her, folding the ticket neatly and tucking it into my pocket. "Although, I'm not an outsider anymore. I live here now. It's my home too."

She scoffs. "No foreigner can truly be at home here. You are a guest. I trust you'll remember that. Have a good day, Miss Orange," Officer Basilier says. I can tell by her tone that she's hoping I have the complete opposite of a good day. Joe and I watch her walk away, our breathing relaxing the moment she's out of sight.

A surprise for the Duke? I think, worry rippling through my limbs.

I lean down to Joe and scratch his head. "Come on, buddy," I tell him. "We've got to warn Jack."

CHAPTER
Thirteen

WHEN JOE and I arrive back at the castle, we check in with Maggie to see if there's any opportunity to meet with the Duke today in an official capacity. "He's in meetings all day," she says, shaking her head. "This port situation in Highland is really out of control. The number of ships being robbed before arrival has doubled. He's tried everything— changing the schedule, speaking with the captains... Our imports are really taking a hit. He's so swamped right now, but I can try to schedule something for tomorrow?"

I tell her not to bother. I'll try to catch Jack later, and— while I don't tell Maggie this— I have an idea of where he'll be.

"Thanks, Maggie," I say with a smile that doesn't quite reach my eyes. As she returns to her mountains of paper-work, I glance down at Joe, who's eyeing me with a look that says he's onto my secret plans. Smart dog.

"Come on, lazybones," I nudge him gently with my foot. "Let's go feed some animals."

Joe perks up at the word 'feed.' We make our way to the animal courtyard, where Alfredo the Giraffe is already peering over his enclosure with those big, hopeful eyes. We give him his dinner, then shuffle over to the zebras, who—unlike Alfredo— maintain a dignified distance until they see the buckets in our hands. "Alright, you stripy rascals, line up," I jest, doling out buckets of food with practiced ease. It's moments like these—simple, peaceful—that make me love my job.

Once everyone's munching happily, Joe gives me a nudge that clearly says: 'What about me?' I roll my eyes but can't help grinning as I dig out a special treat from my pocket. "Here you go, Your Highness," I say, tossing him a piece of cheese. His tail wags a thank you.

With our furry friends fed, it's finally our turn. We head to the dining hall, the scent of roasted vegetables and fresh bread leading us like an invisible leash. The hall buzzes with the soft chatter of staff winding down from their day, and I slide into a seat with a contented sigh. Tonight's dish is a hearty beef stew, and it seems to bring me back to life the way only a good meal can. Maggie doesn't make it to dinner—she's probably too overwhelmed with all the preparation for the festival— so Joe and I enjoy light conversation with the castle's driver, Enrique, and Monique, head of housekeeping.

"The Duke's guest, Frederick, left a horrible mess in his room last night," Monique whispers to me over a bite of bread. "Bottles everywhere. Clothes on the floor. A broken mirror. He is *très terrible*."

"There's only two places he ever asks me to drive him to," Enrique says, placing his hat on the table. "The pub… and the casino."

Once dinner is finished, Joe and I retreat to our apartment. We spend some time looking at our cork-board of potential suspects, then read together on the sofa. As the quiet evening dwindles down, I can't help but look at the clock. I know the Duke will be in the library if he's having a sleepless night, which I imagine is the case, given that he's a suspect in a murder investigation.

Finally, when it's just past midnight, I stretch my arms wide and put Joe into his glitzy new harness. "Do you want to go see Jack?" I ask him. Joe's tail wags at the mention of one of his favorite people.

Together, we step into the brisk night air and cross the courtyard to the castle. It's quiet this late at night, only the sound of crickets singing in the distance. We step off the dew-drenched grass and hop up the castle steps, making our way into the main hallway. Sconces light our path, and we stop when we reach the library, pushing open the heavy, oak door.

A fire crackles in the corner.

There he is, I think, looking at Jack— who's exactly where I knew he'd be this late at night. He's hunched over a desk littered with maps and nautical charts, his silver hair catching the lamplight. The Duke of Atwood doesn't hear us enter; he's absorbed in his research, a frown of concentration etching deeper lines into his forehead.

"Late night," I clear my throat, and his head jerks up.

"You could say that," He smiles at me, not in the least bit surprised to see me. "You're not sleeping either, I see."

"Me, sleep? Never," I say. I step into the library, taking a seat next to the Duke. Joe ambles in behind me and flops down on the ornate rug in front of the fireplace. "My mind kicks into gear after eleven o'clock exactly. What's your excuse?"

"I'm trying to make sense of these thefts at sea," the Duke admits, gesturing at the sea of papers before him. "We've given the captains new security equipment. We've changed the arrivals and departures. But still— these criminals seem to ravage the ships despite our best efforts.

"And there's not a leak?" I suggest considering our last conversation. "A mole, somewhere?"

The Duke takes off his glasses, sighing. "I think there well may be. But proving it or getting the source to own up to it— well, that's another thing. I'm afraid I can't say much.

Monrovian law prevents me from discussing internal affairs with specifics."

"You mean… prevents you from discussing it with someone like me? A foreigner?"

Jack shakes his head. "With anyone at all, I'm afraid."

I seize the moment to ask what's been nagging at me since I spoke to Henri. "Can I ask you something?"

"Anything," the Duke says warmly.

"Why'd you include Rodrigo in the Foundation Festival? He wasn't your biggest fan. Anyone else would have kept him out of the event. Even other vendors didn't want him there"

Jack's expression softens, a blend of sadness and resolve settling on his features. "Monrosha— our founder— had a vision for a Monrovia that was a fair and equitable society," he begins, his voice filled with idealism. "She believed in a world where those in power could be challenged, could be better because of it. Including Rodrigo was...a gesture. An attempt to honor her legacy. He may challenge the public's perception of me, and that may be bad for me— yet good, in its own way, for the country. A free press is important. If leaders aren't challenged, what standards can they be held to?"

"Even if he was writing lies," I press, curious despite myself.

"I certainly wish he'd have chosen the truth," Jack replies, a faint smile playing on his lips. "But not everything he said about me was untrue. There *was* a time I was a playboy on a yacht, as I told you. It was in my youth when I was disillusioned with the monarchy. It's my responsibility to change the public perception of my reputation through action. We grow from criticism. If we silence every dissenting voice, how will we ever learn, ever improve?" He pauses, wondering if he should reveal what's on his mind. He seems to decide he should. "Selfishly, that may have been another reason I invited Rodrigo to be a vendor at the festival. I thought if he saw what I'm trying to do— the effort to serve the people and be transparent— he might come around to the truth about who I am today."

"Spoken like a *true* leader," I say.

"Sometimes I think I'd prefer a good book to leading a Castle," he confesses with a wry chuckle. "But here we are."

"Here we are," I echo. "Jack," I begin, moving on to the real reason I've come to see him tonight. My voice— a low whisper— is still a razor cutting through the hushed stillness of the library, "Officer Basilier has something brewing for you. A surprise, and not the kind that comes with cake and candles."

He looks up, his grey eyes reflecting the moonlight that filters through the tall windows. "Is that so?" he murmurs, setting aside the book with a soft thud.

"Yes," I tuck a stray lock of hair behind my ear. "I've been — I've been investigating—" I say, admitting the truth.

"Of course you have," he sighs. "Rebecca, I don't want a manhunt for me to lead you into a dangerous situation—"

"Don't worry," I sigh. "I'm not getting very far anyway. The villagers don't trust me. It's hard to get people to talk when I'm not a real Monrovian."

"Not a *real* Monrovian?!" Jack says, aghast. "You exhibit every quality Monrovia values. You, Rebecca Orange, are not an outsider. You're one of us. They'll see that soon enough."

"Thanks for the vote of confidence." I give him a wry smile.

Jack stands, crossing to a mahogany bookshelf. He pulls out a volume bound in rich, blue fabric. "This is '*The Founding of Monrovia*'. It details how our country was built by formidable women—leaders like Monrosha, who shaped this land with kindness and iron resolve. People like you."

He passes it to me, and the book feels heavy in my hands. There's the weight of a promise in it, and I realize— for the first time— that Monrovia has become my home. I can't imagine living anywhere else.

"People like *us*," I tell him. "I don't suppose I could convince you to hide somewhere Officer Basilier couldn't find you until the real murderer is discovered? Maybe take a long vacation?"

"That would go about as far with me as my pleas to you to stay out of danger and not investigate Rodrigo's murder," the Duke laughs. "As in, to say— nowhere."

"I guess we both choose our fates, then," I say to him

"My fate tonight is a warm library and excellent company," Jack smiles at me, then returns his gaze to his maps, but not before adding: "Seems I'm a lucky man."

Jack gets back to his work and I settle in beside him, opening up the book about Monrovia's founding. Joe snores gently from his resting place. The fireplace crackles and— even though I'm afraid of what's coming— this moment, all on its own— is perfect. There's nothing better than finding a person you're comfortable being silent around. The hours tick by in peaceful quiet, and for once, I feel like I'm right where I belong. It's as if I'm in a safe cocoon, where nothing— *nothing* — bad could ever happen.

CHAPTER
Fourteen

"SOMETHING BAD HAS HAPPENED," Maggie blurts out, her face paler than the walls of the staff dining hall. I'm mid-sip of my morning salvation—a double-shot latte with just a hint of vanilla— but her abrupt appearance makes me nearly choke on the frothy goodness.

"Define 'bad,'" I say, setting down my cup and brushing crumbs from my half-devoured sesame bagel onto Joe, who's lounging at my feet. He doesn't seem to mind; in fact, he looks rather pleased with the unexpected shower of breakfast treats.

"Officer Basilier has brought charges against the Duke," Maggie exclaims in a hushed, frightened tone.

"Already?" I can't mask the disbelief—or is it fear?—in my voice. I glance down at Joe, searching for some canine wisdom, but he's too busy being a four-legged vacuum cleaner. "I thought we had some time! It's too soon. What evidence does she have? Someone has to intervene!"

"Come on." Maggie grabs my arm, pulling me up from the table so fast my chair almost tips over. Joe, sensing the urgency (or maybe just hoping for more food), follows suit, his tail swishing.

Maggie leads us out of the staff building and into the courtyard, the morning air crisp on my skin. We tread across the grassy opening toward the castle, then make our way up the steps into the ancient building. Joe and I follow Maggie through the castle corridors— dripping with grandeur and history— finally stopping at a room I recognize as Maggie's office. Maggie has a huge job managing all the needs of the castle, and her office reflects both the legacy of her position, as well as contemporary demands. It's a cozy clash of medieval and modern, with personal knick-knacks nestled among the tech and tasteful décor. Tiny stuffed animals dot the window, along with a jump-rope, which Maggie has told me is her favorite form of exercise.

On a bookshelf in the corner, a TV blares a news report. Reporters hold microphones up to a familiar figure standing in front of the Atwood Village Police Department. Officer Basilier's stone-cold face fills the screen.

"In the issue of Rodrigo Harlton's murder, charges against the Duke of Atwood will be formally presented," Officer Basilier announces, her voice cutting through the air in a way that sends chills down my spine. She smiles as she delivers the news, positively gleeful at the idea of hurting Jack, who's never done anything to wrong her. For a moment, a surge of anger at Officer Basilier waves through my stomach, but I push it away. Now is the time to stay calm. I can't help the Duke if I don't hold it together myself. "My office would like the public to know that the Duke of Atwood has been wholly cooperative during our investigation, and has agreed to turn himself in for processing at the Village courthouse by 11 a.m."

"Turn himself in?" I echo, incredulous. My gaze flicks to the digital clock sitting by Maggie's computer. It's fifteen minutes until eleven.

"Following bail posting, the Duke will be released while he awaits a trial," the officer continues, her tone dripping a smugness that sends another wave of rage through my system. "I'll open it up to any questions?" Officer Basilier says to the reporters, licking her lips.

A dozen hands go up. Officer Basilier points at a woman in the front row, who's holding a microphone toward her. The reporter jumps at the chance to ask her question.

"What evidence has led the Police to bring charges against the Duke? Do you feel you have a strong case?"

"We certainly feel that justice will be served," Officer Basilier says, nodding. "But as to what led us to bring charges — the investigation made a significant breakthrough with the discovery of a handkerchief at the crime scene, emblazoned with the Royal insignia."

"A *handkerchief*?" I say out loud, throwing my hands up in the air. "Jack doesn't even carry handkerchiefs! Have you ever seen him use one?" I ask Maggie, who shakes her head.

"Never," Maggie agrees. "He may be a Duke, but he's not a Duke in the 1800s. Jack uses a tissue like everyone else."

My feet move of their own accord, taking me in circles around the room. Joe follows me, his toenails clicking against the ancient hardwood floors, and together we pace through the possibilities. "We were there the morning Rodrigo was found and I didn't see a handkerchief anywhere around the scene of the crime. We interviewed Jocelyn after the Police cleaned it up and she didn't say a thing. If Officer Basilier had found the handkerchief right after the murder she would have brought charges against Jack right away. That means…" I pause, considering the implications. "That means she must have found the handkerchief later. Or even *placed* it there."

"You think she's setting the Duke up?" Maggie asks, aghast at the idea.

I squint at the TV, picturing Jack—the guy more likely to discuss Proust than party plans— reporting to the Police Station for processing.

"All I know is that something doesn't add up. And the

only people looking out for Jack are the three of us in this room…" Maggie nods, her braids bouncing in agreement.

"He's innocent," she says firmly. "We've got to clear his name."

A glance at the clock shakes me out of my musings. It's five minutes to eleven a.m.

I bolt from the chair, nearly knocking it over as my heart races in my chest. "We've got to stop Jack from reporting to the station! He just lends credibility to the charges if he does. He should make a press announcement. Renounce all of this—"

Maggie's next words hit me like a ton of bricks. "He's already gone, Rebecca. Enrique's driving him to the station."

"Already?" My voice pitches up into a note of panic that even Joe seems to pick up on, his golden ears perking with concern. I waste no time; action is needed, and fast. Dashing across the room, I shove the heavy door open and sprint down the corridor, Joe lumbering behind me with an unenthusiastic huff. The thought of Jack, alone with his thoughts on such a drive, makes me run even faster.

The cool breeze outside slaps my face as I emerge from the castle and rush down the front steps. My eyes scan the grounds just in time to catch the tail end of a black SUV rolling past the iron gates. Outside the security of the gates, reporters swarm, cameras flashing, hoping for a statement, a scandal—anything. It looks as if every reporter in the country of Monrovia has decided to descend upon the Village of Atwood.

"Jack!" I yell pointlessly, knowing he can't hear me. Joe barks once, echoing my frustration. The car disappears, and just as quickly as it arrived— the moment is gone.

"Rebecca, wait!" Maggie's voice floats from behind me, her breath short from trying to keep up.

I turn back to her, flushed from the sprint. "We have to go after him," I say, determination lacing my tone.

"He told me not to intervene—"

"He's just being brave," I say, waving a hand in the air. "Jack doesn't want any of us to get into trouble trying to help him. But he needs us. If it were anyone on our staff, Jack would go to the jail himself to get them out."

Maggie considers this, then nods. "Walk to Atwood?" Maggie asks, looking down the road.

"Enrique's got the only car, and we can't exactly summon a royal carriage," I quip half-heartedly.

"Right. Let's go," Maggie agrees. Her usually bubbly demeanor has flattened in a firm line. Maggie has been working for the Duke for years and tells me he's the best boss she's ever had. She feels the same sense of loyalty I do, although mine may be laced with something deeper than friendship.

Joe ambles up beside us, looking between Maggie and me. His ears are flattened to his head, his eyebrows tilting to the side to express his concern. When I start walking, he follows loyally without even needing a treat to coerce him down the path to help his best friend.

With the castle receding in the distance, we step onto the cobblestone path, none of us quite sure of *how* we plan on helping the Duke— only that we're going to try.

CHAPTER
Fifteen

THE MOMENT we step into the police station, it's like entering a whole new world—sterile and imposing, not at all like the cozy, book-lined nooks of Monrovia Castle or the cheery bustle of the Village of Atwood. Maybe we've arrived in time to stop the Duke from turning himself in. But even if we haven't, I plan to be here when he's released.

Maggie looks around the Police Station, twirling one of her braids in her hand. Joe whimpers beside me. I wonder if he can smell that the Duke has already been here. Just then, Joe sniffs the air and whines, flopping on to the floor beside me.

"I see the Royal Reception team has arrived. I imagine you'll be rolling out the red carpet when the Duke is released?"

There she is, Officer Basilier, standing guard behind the counter like it's her personal fortress. Her arms are crossed over her chest and— on the other side of the counter, seated in a chair— is the Duke, his mouth open in alarm at the sight of us. My shoulders relax and I'm relieved to see him— until I notice he's handcuffed to the chair.

"Rebecca!" Jack exclaims, alarmed. "You shouldn't be here. And Maggie, I explicitly told you *not* to intervene—"

"We wanted to make sure you were okay," Maggie says. She looks as alarmed as I am to see the Duke in such a state. "I've made a call to the King and Queen," she continues, her speech quickening as an Officer takes the Duke's fingerprints. "They're going to call the Castle lawyers—"

"The Duke has been read his rights and knows what he's entitled to," Officer Basilier interjects. "Unless the two of you have a crime to report, I'll ask you to wait outside." She motions at the doors from which we just entered the building.

"Take Rebecca back to the castle," Jack shouts to Maggie as another Officer un-handcuffs him from the chair, leading him down a long hallway toward an area out of sight. "That's an official order!"

"It's her day off," Maggie shouts back, smiling a little. "Neither one of us can obey official orders on the weekend. Sorry!"

Despite himself, Jack smiles a little as he's led down the hallway for further processing. His good-natured humor in the face of adversity makes me even angrier at Officer Basilier for what she's done.

I step forward, closing the distance between myself and Officer Basilier with a stride that I hope conveys more confidence than I feel. "The Duke is innocent," I say, keeping my voice steady despite the flutter in my chest. "The real murderer is out there, and you're letting them get away— all because you're so focused on one man."

"Is that so, Ms. Orange?" Officer Basilier retorts, her eyebrow raising a single inch.

"I don't know what you *think* you found," I say "But that handkerchief wasn't there the morning Maggie and I discovered Rodrigo's body," I say, lowering my voice an octave. "I would've seen it. And I'll testify to that in court."

Officer Basilier leans forward on the counter, her eyes

boring into mine. "People tend to see what they want when nobility is involved."

"All the Duke wants is to be treated like everyone else," I say. "But you won't give him that. You're going to parade him around like a trophy, and when everyone figures out that you're letting a real murderer run loose on the streets just because of your prejudice, there's going to be hell to pay. I *will* solve this crime," I tell her, really meaning it. "And when I do, the same thing that happened to Cadet Monroe is going to happen to you. You'll be finished. Mark my words."

I turn on my heel, and Maggie and Joe follow me out of the police station onto the cobblestone streets of the village.

"Rebecca!" Maggie yells after me. I should stop but I don't. I'm not thinking straight. I'm too angry. My legs carry me to the fountain that sits in the center of the Village's court-yard. I perch on the edge of its basin, inhaling deeply as the sound of trickling water brings me back down to Earth. Joe leaps onto the edge of the fountain and sits beside me, his golden fur warm against my skin. He licks my face— a favorite move of his that he uses when he can tell that I'm going through something.

"Rebecca, you just threatened a Police Officer," Maggie says, out of breath. She puts her hands on her knees, trying to steady herself.

"I know, I know," I say, my heart pounding. "It was stupid. It was a dumb move. It was—"

"*Awesome!*" Maggie says, pumping a fist in the air. "I wish I'd gotten it on video. Her mouth was all open like a fish. And when you said '*you'll be finished!*'" Maggie offers an impression of me that depicts a warrior, hand up in the air. "Her cheeks got red! It was the greatest thing I've ever seen."

"Hope you still think it's great when I'm sitting in a jail cell next to the Duke."

Maggie waves a hand in the air as if to say my possible imprisonment is nothing but a minor detail. "She would need a cause for that. You haven't broken any laws I'm aware of. At least, not yet."

There's a whistle from across the courtyard, and the three of us look up to discover Enrique, the castle driver. He's leaning against the black SUV that's parked outside the Police Station, awaiting the Duke's release. He walks over to us, unbothered by the day's traumatic events.

"*Bonjour*," He says, smiling at us. "It's a beautiful day despite all of this, no?" He motions back toward the village. "Should we grab a pastry while we wait for the Duke?"

"Enrique," I say, shaking my head. "The Duke is getting released on bail. Not running some errands at the local market. How can you think about food at a time like this?"

"Easy," Enrique says, shrugging. "The Duke can handle any difficulty. I am confident in his resolve. And, beyond that, that smell from *Le Petit Scone* wafts this way. What's a man to do?"

"Enrique," Maggie clucks her tongue at him.

"*Non, mon ami,*" Enrique smiles at me. "The truth is, I know the Duke will be alright because Miss Rebecca Orange is investigating. And— although she might not have been born here in Monrovia— the moment she arrived, I saw that she possessed Monrovian spirit. She will use her courage to get to the bottom of this. I have no doubt. Until then— pastries."

Enrique puts his arm around my shoulder, and the four of us— Enrique, Maggie, Joe, and me— head toward Henri's bakery. As we walk, we pass the statue of Monrosha, looming over us with a promise in her eyes that says she will make sure the Duke is redeemed.

A few hours later and the Duke is released on bail. We pick

him up at the Police Station, his hair a little mussed, but otherwise no worse for wear.

"I must say, jail is a transformative place," the Duke teases us in the Village Courtyard. "I've emerged a new man. Fully changed."

"You were locked up for three hours," Enrique rolls his eyes.

"I notice there's no press," Jack looks around, relieved. "Such a feat seems impossible."

"Maggie spent this entire time on the phone with every reporter in Monrovia," I say, proud of my friend. "She planted a false story that they'd transferred you to another station. They all bought it hook, line, and sinker."

"Well, almost all of them—" Maggie says, nodding across the way to the newsstand. There, Zacharia has his cell phone out. He's taking frantic pictures of the Duke, a huge smile plastered on his face. "I figured if someone was going to get an exclusive scoop, it might as well be one of Atwood's own."

"Truly patriotic of you," Jack smiles. "Rebecca, Maggie," he says, his voice a smooth melody. "Your support today has been invaluable. I'm indebted to both of you. Enrique—" He looks at the driver, misty-eyed. "I must ask you a serious question." He pauses, somber. "Is what's in that bag for me?"

Enrique holds up a paper to-go bag from *Le Petit Scone*. "Three cream-filled pastries. Just for you." He passes it to the Duke, who breathes a sigh of relief as he gets in the car. "What would I do, without such good people in my life?"

As the Duke and Enrique get into the SUV, I think about how the castle would change without the Duke. Before his arrival, it was a place of toil. Now, it's a place of equanimity and friendship. I'm not going to let Officer Basilier scare us into stopping the investigation. Whoever killed Rodrigo has also put the Duke's future— and mine, and the Castle's— at risk. And no matter who it is— no matter where they are— I'm going to find them.

The Duke rolls down his window. "Rebecca?" He says, concerned. "Aren't you and Maggie coming? And Joe, of course?"

He motions for us to hop into the car, but instead, we share a glance. I can tell from Maggie's expression that she already knows what I'm thinking.

"Thanks," I say, "But we have a mystery to solve."

The Duke's eyes narrow in protest. "You can't possibly still intend to—"

Maggie thumps the hood of the SUV twice. "Enrique! The Duke has a video meeting on his calendar with the King and Queen. Quite the important call, so let's speed it up?"

At her orders, Enrique pulls the SUV out of its parking spot. The Duke rolls down his window, calling after us, but before he can protest further— they're driving out of sight, leaving the village behind.

"Where to now?" Maggie asks me, reaching down to pat Joe's furry head.

"We're going to talk to the only person who might know how the handkerchief appeared."

Sixteen

AS JOE, Maggie, and I push open the door to *Cafe de Flore*, the smell of coffee and flowers greets us like a hug. Books line the walls as if the very structure were built on literature itself. Flowers cascade from every conceivable nook, turning the cafe into a garden sanctuary. A corner table hosts a group of patrons sipping on coffees. I'm reminded why I love this place, and— for a second— forget that it was the scene of Rodrigo's murder. Beside me, Joe seems less concerned with the decor and more interested in the potential for crumbs beneath the tables, his nose twitching with each new scent.

We find Jocelyn behind the counter, artfully arranging a bouquet in a vase. Her kind smile is comforting, even before she speaks. When she spots us, there's no tone of surprise in her voice. "I figured it was only a matter of time until you'd come knocking again." Her brown hair is tucked neatly behind her ears, and she avoids looking at me.

"I need to know—" I begin to say.

"About the handkerchief," Jocelyn nods, finally meeting my gaze. She reaches under the counter and removes a pitcher of amber-colored liquid, pouring it into three glasses

— two of which she slides toward Maggie and me. "Petal perfection iced tea," she says. "It's rose, lavender, peaches, and chamomile." She starts to come around the counter, then thinks better of it, pausing to remove a bone for Joe out of a glass jar. "We keep these for when guests bring their pets," she smiles, luring Joe toward a table. The three of us take a seat, undisturbed in the corner.

I take a sip of the tea. It's like nothing I've ever tasted. A fruity-floral mix of peach and rose.

"Things had finally started to feel normal again," Jocelyn begins in a soft voice. She sounds almost relieved to talk to us about what she knows. "The police had finished their inspection. Business was back to usual. This nightmare was over... or so I thought."

"Until?" Maggie prompts.

"Officer Basilier returned two days ago." Jocelyn pauses, the strain in her eyes hinting at mixed emotions. "She said an anonymous tip brought her back to the scene of the crime. I hate to think that's what my beautiful cafe has become—" she motions around the space. "'The *scene* of a crime.'" She takes another sip of her tea.

"What did the anonymous tip say?" I ask, leaning forward, my curiosity piqued.

"Whoever it was told her that the murderer left something in the bookshelf next to the area where Rodrigo...you know..." She trails off. Her gaze flickers toward the bookshelf in question. It's a simple one, lined with tomes of different colors and weights. "She had her team tear the entire shelf apart. They weren't exactly gentle with my collection. It took me all night to get the shelves back in order. She made her officers go through each book page by page. In one of them... tucked between bent pages... they found the handkerchief with the Royal insignia."

"And she seriously thinks that's evidence?" Maggie asks,

throwing her hands in the air. "What kind of murderer would kill somebody then leave a handkerchief behind— hidden in a book— to incriminate themselves?"

"She supposes the Duke I guess," Jocelyn shrugs. "It doesn't make sense to me, either."

"Which book was it in?" I ask, leaning forward. My mind starts racing through possibilities. A clue hidden in literature could point to a very literate criminal—or a very stupid one.

"It was a book about the Royal Family and Monrovian law," Jocelyn replies, the lineup of spines. There, in between other legal-looking titles, sits a thick book with gold writing on the exterior— *Monrovian Law and the Monarchy: An In-Depth Analysis.*

"Have you seen anyone loitering around here? Maybe someone particularly interested in that section?" I keep my tone light, but my brain is whirring.

"No, nothing like that. Nobody ever goes near that shelf," Jocelyn says. "Fiction is our most popular area. The legal shelf is hardly ever touched. If somebody *had* looked at it, I would have noticed, considering how strange I'd find it!"

"Then the handkerchief must have been placed there before the murder was even committed," I conclude. "And someone who knew it was there called Officer Basilier to offer an anonymous tip. Or, maybe, they slipped past Jocelyn after the murder and left the handkerchief there to frame the Duke. Have you left the store alone at all?"

Jocelyn nods. "I take Mondays off. I have a girl who takes over for me. She doesn't keep as close an eye on things as I do. It's very possible someone could have slipped the hand-kerchief into the book unnoticed."

"Do you mind if I take the book?" I ask, tilting my head towards the shelf. Jocelyn's eyes flicker with something unreadable before she nods and stands, removing the book from the shelf and passing it to me.

"Of course," she murmurs softly, her fingers brushing the aged cover as she hands it over to me. "I'm sorry about all this mess with the Duke," she adds, a hint of genuine regret lacing her words. "But when the police come knocking, what can I do but let them in?"

"We understand," I reply, clutching the book. "Thank you again for helping us." I try to offer a reassuring smile, all the while nodding at Maggie that it's time to leave.

"Thanks for everything," Maggie says. "This was great." She smiles at her finished iced tea. Joe wags his tail, sensing the shift in mood as we make our way out of the quaint café.

The air outside is brisk as we commence our stroll back to the castle. Joe trots alongside us, his golden coat gleaming in the afternoon sun.

"Jocelyn was cooperative, but—"

"What if she offered the anonymous tip and planted the handkerchief?" Maggie finishes my thought for me. "She *does* have access to the cafe 24/7. And she had a motivation for wanting Rodrigo dead because of his bad reviews. So it's possible she killed him and tried to frame the Duke for the crime. But I just don't picture her as—"

"A murderer?" I ask. "Neither do I."

Maggie glances at me, her brows knitting together in concern. "But those handkerchiefs are super rare," she says, pulling up an image on her phone. The intricately embroidered fabric glows on the screen, a testament to a bygone era of royal opulence. "I looked it up earlier today. They're only owned by the Royals or those they've favored with a gift."

"Which means someone with access to those circles must be involved..."

"I don't even know how Jocelyn could have accessed such a thing," Maggie says. "Although she does see a ton of people come through the cafe. Maybe she traded for it or got it as a present. Half of those books are rare editions, and she's pretty involved in the antique market. She might know some people who have access to all kinds of interesting objects."

"But why set up the Duke?" I shrug, still unable to make sense of the mess. "Jocelyn doesn't have anything against him."

I clutch the book tighter to my chest. I'm not familiar with Monrovian law, but whoever placed that handkerchief in the book was reading it for a reason. And I intend to find out what that reason was. Whatever lies within these pages, it's bound to bring us closer to the truth.

———

When we get to the castle, Maggie and I break off to attend to our separate chores for the day. She heads back to her office, while Joe and I make our way to visit the animals in the courtyard for some light training and feeding.

I'm in the middle of my daily ritual— doling out feed to a row of expectant zebras— when the quiet is pierced by a sniffle. I turn around to find Penny— the Duke's guest— dabbing at her eyes with a handkerchief that looks like it belongs in a museum—or a crime scene.

My heart races as I recognize the Royal insignia on the fabric. It's just like the picture Maggie showed me. The handkerchief is a perfect copy of the one found at the crime scene.

"Penny?" I wave at her, and for the first time, she notices Joe and I standing behind a hay bale. "Everything okay?

She looks up, trying to muster a smile through her tears. "Oh, Rebecca, I just—" She sighs, quickly arranging her expression into something neutral. "I'm afraid the moment just caught up with me."

"Anything we can do?" I ask. Joe and I walk toward her, standing beside her beneath the shade of a tree.

"It's nothing," she says, waving the idea away. "I came to

my brother with an idea to address the situation happening at the ports in Highland and he was quite cross with me."

"I noticed he can be..." I pause, afraid to say the wrong thing.

"He *can* be," she nods. "I'm quite frustrated with myself for crying over it all. Being Royal may look wonderful and I'm certainly grateful for my status, but— as I believe Jack demonstrated today— to be Royal is merely to have the illusion of power. Not the truth of it." She wipes her nose with the back of the handkerchief. "Good people face hard fates, while those like my brother gamble away their legacy. I only wish I could make this country better."

"You can," I say.

"Not any more than an ordinary citizen, I'm afraid," she smiles at me gently. "My brother was born first. And so, the title is his. He is in charge and I'm just an ordinary citizen with a meaningless title and the opportunity to bend his ear. But— like any ordinary citizen— I do what I can in my own little way. I plead for those cases I care about. I donate to causes that I believe will make the world better. That's all one can do, yes?"

"Yes," I agree."

She pats my arm. "Thank you, Rebecca. For the chat, I mean. But I really should get back—" She nods at the castle. "My brother has failed to show up for yet another call about the ports. It seems it is left to me to lead by proxy. There's little I can approve without his official approval, but I'll still try to help the situation anyway."

"All the work and none of the credit," I say.

"Who needs credit?" Penny smiles gently. "As long as what needs to be done is done."

With that, she heads back for the castle, her shoulders straight in the face of a difficult afternoon. It strikes me as unfair that her brother— Frederick— gets the title of Duke of Highland only because he was born first. I scratch Joe's ears, more thankful than ever for people like Penny and Jack who make me believe in the good within us all.

Seeing Penny with the handkerchief feels important, although I can't say why. An idea seems to skirt around the edges of my mind, but I can't quite grab it. Still, I tuck the information away, hoping answers will come.

CHAPTER
Seventeen

IT'S the day of the Foundation Festival. I'm up with the sun, which is a rare treat—or punishment, depending on how many cups of coffee it takes to get my gears turning. Usually the castle is quiet this early in the morning, but today, the place buzzes with activity. The Foundation Festival is just a few hours away, and it's all hands on deck to make the event happen.

"Joe," I call out, but as usual, my faithful Tibetan Mastiff merely raises an eyebrow from his cozy spot in the sun-drenched corner of the main castle courtyard. I chuckle to myself and leave him be; there's work to be done.

Maggie is already bustling about, her blonde braids bouncing as she directs the staff with a clipboard in hand. "Rebecca! Isn't this exciting?" Her voice rings out clear and jubilant across the courtyard. I can't help but smile at her enthusiasm—it's infectious.

"It became way more exciting after Joe and I grabbed some warm coffee from the French press Chef Renauld left out," I smile at her.

A group of staff members pass us, carrying tables and

chairs. "Let's get those tables over by the western wall!" Maggie calls out to them, pointing to where the shadows will provide respite from the midday sun. The staff nods and begins arranging the furniture according to her instructions, heavy oak tables gliding across the grass as if they were part of an elaborate ballroom routine.

"When the castle gates open for the villagers, I just want everything to be perfect," Maggie says, letting out a sigh. "Their view of the castle hasn't exactly improved since the Duke's arrest…"

"How's he doing?" I say, trying not to let on that I'm disappointed I haven't heard from Jack in the past couple of days.

"He's been hiding," Maggie says, an arch in her eyebrow telling me she might have picked up on my disappointment. "He's trying to keep a low profile and avoid dragging anyone else into the mess he's in. I checked his calendar and it's booked with calls to the Royal Family's attorneys. Thankfully, the King and Queen have been supportive. They know Jack isn't a murderer, and they understand what it's like to be unfairly targeted."

"That's great," I say, still unable to shake my concern.

Maggie touches my arm. "He told me to focus on getting the Festival ready. He said the town needs it."

"Then let's do it," I offer her a weak smile. Beside us, a statue of Monrosha is wheeled toward the common area. It's a carbon copy of the one in the village. Her posture is noble, and the basket of bread she's holding is carved to perfection. We watch as the staff positions the statue near a banner that reads "Foundation Festival."

"How can we allow such injustice?" Maggie sighs, looking at the statue. "When our founder was a woman who gave up her last piece of bread for the people?"

"I don't know," I shake my head. "Jack should be here. He shouldn't have to hide."

"Right you are, Rebecca," a voice echoes out behind me. I turn, discovering the Duke of Atwood. He steps forward and takes my hand, kissing the back of it with a slight bow. "And here I am, ready to help." He holds out his arms and rolls up his sleeves. He's dressed casually as if prepared to do manual labor. I've never seen him this way, and he still looks good, if not— lost— outside of his more formal button-down shirts. "Maggie?" He says, smiling. "Put me to work."

"You're sure—"

"I am," the Duke insists. "I need a distraction and physical labor is just the ticket."

After Maggie points him in the right direction, the Duke joins a team of staff members putting together a giant, white tent that will cover all of the food offerings. Meanwhile, Maggie and I make plans for the petting zoo.

"This is perfect. It's flat enough the animals will feel comfortable, and there's enough space for them to maneuver," I say, motioning to a generous patch of grass near the courtyard's biggest fountain. I envision little hands reaching out to stroke the soft fur of alpacas and the odd stripes of zebras. I can't wait to see the kids' eyes light up when they're introduced to the animals.

"Perfect!" Maggie says. She kneels down and starts outlining the space with a temporary blue spray paint. "I'll have the staff get started on installing the fence. Zebras and alpacas, oh, the children will love it!"

"Can't forget about the treats for our four-legged stars," I add with a wink. "I've purchased two big bags of the best feed from Benjamin, so hopefully the animals will be motivated to interact. Maybe Joe, too," I laugh, looking at Joe, who's still sleeping under a tree. If I know my dog, he'll be first in line if there's food involved. I shake my head at the thought of him trying to blend in among the zebras in hopes of snagging a snack.

Maggie laughs, her voice mingling with the clatter of the

preparations, and I join in. Today is about community, history, and a touch of animal magic. And I wouldn't have it any other way.

Once the fence for the petting zoo is outlined, Maggie and I make our way to the section of the courtyard that's been earmarked for the vendors. Four quaint booths have already been assembled in the space, and the vendors are here setting up their wares.

Henri, in his flour-dusted apron, nods at me as he arranges an array of delicate scones and croissants on a pastel tablecloth. "*Bonjour*, Rebecca! Ready to taste the magic?" he asks, with an unusual twinkle in his eye. *Maybe the brusk baker is starting to like me,* I think. Is it possible? But before I can entertain the idea, he adds: "Even someone who's not a *real* Monrovian— like you— can appreciate our traditional pastry!" He motions around the table at the snacks.

"Gee, thanks, Henri. I appreciate that," I shake my head, sure that he doesn't notice the sarcasm.

Next to Henri's booth, Benjamin from Indiana Bones is wrestling a roll-up banner of a dashing dog wearing a fedora.

"Need a hand?" I ask, stepping in to steady the stand.

"Thanks, Rebecca. This banner is giving me more trouble than the puppies at yesterday's obedience class!" His words are tinged with amusement as he meticulously lays out a treasure trove of pet goodies: leashes, treats, even tiny fedoras. A cheeky nod to his American movie hero, no doubt.

"Indy would be proud," I say, earning a wink from Benjamin. Out of everyone in the Village, Benjamin has been especially welcoming to Joe and me, maybe because his favorite movie is American.

A sweet smell clings to the air and I walk toward it— trancelike. It's coming from the next booth, which belongs to Jocelyn and *Cafe de Flore*. At the booth, Jocelyn arranges her coffee oasis with floral precision. "Rebecca, try the new 'rose ripple' latte," she insists, pouring a delicate stream of pink froth into a cup adorned with petals.

"Sounds divine, but later, okay? I had three cups of coffee just to get up this early," I say, my resolve nearly crumbling at the sight of her coffee creations.

"Later, then," she replies, her smile as warm as the steam wafting from her espresso machine.

At the last booth— Zacharia— from the newsstand, arranges magazines. His booth is plastered with headlines. One in particular snags my gaze—the latest issue of *Monrovia Gossip*, the Duke of Atwood's face splashed across the front alongside the words '*The Murderous Monarch: The Duke of Atwood Declared Murder Suspect*.' It's Rodrigo's legacy in print form.

"Zacharia, this is quite the headline," I say, picking up a copy.

"Hey," he shrugs. "I gotta report on it whether it's good or bad."

"I'd expect nothing less," I say, hoping he'll think to report on the success of the Foundation Festival and everything the castle has done to make the event happen.

"I do miss Rodrigo," Zacharia says, his eyes suddenly watering. "And for whatever it's worth, I don't think the Duke is guilty."

"You don't?"

"No," Zacharia shakes his head. "Rodrigo had a lotta enemies. It's a consequence of the job. He hung out with shady characters. Even the latest story— the one he was so excited about right before he died?— he got that tip from some underground Blackjack game. Apparently the dealer was drinking on the job and made a bet with him. Said if Rodrigo won the hand instead of the house, he'd tell him a scoop he got from another player a couple of nights before. Something about the Royals. Sure enough, Rodrigo won the hand. He never failed when a story was at stake," Zacharia wipes his eyes at the memory.

"Hardly the most reliable source," I muse, realizing I've just been given new information that— for reasons yet unknown to me— feels important.

He got the tip from the Blackjack table, I think, willing my brain to tell me something that my spirit already knows. *Why does that feel important?* The words don't come, and I catalog the information for later.

"He'd have loved to have been here," Zacharia says, sniffling a little.

I put a hand on his shoulder. "He'd be glad to have passed the torch to you," I say, trying my best not to be angry about the magazine cover of the Duke. Zacharia is just doing his best to carry on the business— and the story, while annoying — is true. The Duke is a murder suspect— but not a murderer. I tuck the magazine under my arm and step away from Zacharia's booth. Maggie waves at me from across the courtyard, but I'm only half there, my mind chewing on an idea that refuses to fully form.

"Earth to Rebecca," Maggie teases, snapping her fingers in front of my face. "You look like you've seen a ghost or—worse —a hungry zebra."

"I'm thinking about what Zacharia just said... something about Rodrigo and his questionable sources." My eyes drift to the castle towers above us, feeling the weight of history—and mystery—in their silent watch.

"Sounds like a typical gossip reporter to me," Maggie shrugs, dismissing the concern as she hands me a stack of program flyers. "Probably another one of his fake stories."

"Maybe," I agree, though doubt pinches at my insides. "Let's get these programs put out on the tables," I say, redirecting my focus to the task at hand. My gut tells me this puzzle piece doesn't fit just yet, but I file it away in the cabinet of curiosities that is my mind.

"Lead the way," Maggie says with a grin, and together we dive back into the flurry of festival preparations. But in the back of my mind, Rodrigo's drunken blackjack dealer continues to deal cards I can't quite read.

CHAPTER
Eighteen

IT'S FINALLY HERE. The Foundation Festival bursts to life, and I'm right in the thick of it. The castle courtyard is a patchwork of stalls and laughter. Villagers mill about, filling the space to the brim. Douglas has planted vibrant new flowers, and offers a tour of the vegetable gardens to a group of villagers. Nearby, Tracey leads a free pilates class out on the grass. There's an energy in the air that's made all the preparation worth it— a shared excitement that knits the community together. Citizens from not just the Village of Atwood, but from all over Monrovia have arrived, bringing an enthusiasm usually reserved for royal weddings.

In the middle of the crowd, I spot Jack— the Duke of Atwood— ducking behind a stall as a gaggle of reporters swarm past, notepads at the ready. His grey hair glints under the sun, wrinkles by his eyes deepening with a smile that says he'd much rather be discussing the enlightenment philosopher John Locke over a pint than dodging scandalous questions. Maggie asked him earlier if he was sure he wanted to attend given his most recent scandal, and he insisted that he wouldn't shirk his Royal Duties. He catches my eye as he dodges the reporters, winking at me and disappearing into the catering tent.

I return my attention to the petting zoo. Joe and I are showing a group of kids around the animal pen. "He won't hurt you," I coax, gesturing to the zebra, whose stripes look painted on by some divine hand. A little girl in front of me looks skeptical. "You can pet him," I tell her. "Just be gentle." She pets the zebra and other kids join in. Their little hands reach out with care, and I imagine every one of them growing up to be an animal trainer.

At the edge of the pen, a familiar face appears: it's Officer Basilier, her gaze sweeping over the animal pen like a hawk. She catches my eye and gives me a nod so curt it could sever a thread. Still, a nod's a nod, and I'll take it.

"Rebecca," she says. "I see you've met my daughter."

I glance at the little girl petting the zebra. *Who knew?* I think. Officer Basilier has a daughter.

"She'll make a great future animal trainer," I tell the Officer, who can't help but smile. She takes her daughter's hand and they disappear into the crowd.

I look down at Joe, who's sprawled out beside the alpacas, soaking up attention like sunlight. Kids flock to him, burying their hands in his gold mane. They almost seem more interested in Joe than the exotic animals. "How much does he weigh?" A little boy asks me as he pets Joe's tail.

"More than me!" I say. The little boy giggles.

I toss Joe a piece of cheese from my training fanny pack, and he bites it down in one gulp. "Show-off," I mutter, but I can't hide my grin.

"Rebecca!" The voice pulls me from my thoughts, and I turn to see Penny, vibrant as ever, with Frederick in tow. He's glancing at his watch like it's a lifeline, eyes darting down to his wrist.

"Thank you for showing us around the other day," Penny says, her gratitude genuine. "These animals are so healing."

"Anything for a friend," I reply, though my eyes are on Frederick, who's practically bouncing on his toes. "You must have a busy schedule today?" I ask.

"We're heading back to Highland today," Frederick answers. "As soon as possible, actually."

"There's the situation at the ports to address—" Penny starts to say, but Frederick talks over her.

"Can't wait to hit a *real* casino," he says under his breath. "The opportunities for a good time are— limited— in such a small village as Atwood. Highland has much more to offer a man."

I bite my tongue, annoyed to see a grown man so antsy to throw his money away. "Good luck then," I say, though in my head I'm adding *'you'll need it'*.

Frederick has just enough patience to allow Penny to pet a zebra, and then the pair takes off. Penny mouths the words "thank you" over her shoulder at me as they blend into the crowd, headed to the castle gates.

I watch them go, noting Penny's warm smile and Frederick's fidgety departure. It's only once they're out of sight that it hits me.

A chill of realization trickles down my spine.

Frederick.

The gambling.

Rodrigo's last scoop— the one he was killed over— was from a Blackjack dealer, I think.

Suddenly, the pieces fall into place. I think about the ripped headline found in Rodrigo's hand and what it said:

"The Crown Doesn't Belong on His Head."

I know who killed Rodrigo. And as it turns out, Officer Basilier wasn't completely wrong: the murderer *is* a Royal. But not the Duke of Atwood.

"Joe," I whisper, urgency in my voice. "We've got to hustle."

Joe lifts his head, sensing the shift in my tone. He shakes off his lazy attitude as he scrambles to his paws, ready for action. "Kids, everyone out! The petting zoo will reopen in an hour, but for now, we're closed!" The kids let out sounds of disappointment as they evacuate the space. I make sure the fence is locked to keep the zebras in check, then get moving.

"Come on, buddy," I say to Joe, breaking into a run. We weave through clusters of festival-goers, past the vendor stalls and the scent of cinnamon clinging to the air. Finally, we spot Maggie, standing by the catering tent.

"Rebecca? Are you okay—" Maggie says as we near her.

"Frederick!" is all I manage between breaths. "Murder... Duke... framed!"

"Slow down, Rebecca." Maggie's eyes widen, her hands fluttering. "What about Frederick?"

"Killed Rodrigo," I say, panting, "and pinned it on the Duke. He's leaving—now!"

Maggie's face flushes as she realizes I've solved the case. "Frederick? The Duke of Highland?" She says, the pieces falling into place. "But he's leaving today. I booked their plane tickets." She checks her watch. "We have to stop them — Let's go!"

Together, we sprint across the dew-kissed grass, Joe keeping pace with surprising agility for a creature whose favorite hobby is napping in sunbeams.

"Stop!" I shout as we near the gates. A guard is about to open them, and Frederick and Penny are standing before him — just an inch away from freedom.

Frederick turns, and the moment he makes eye contact with me, it's clear he knows I'm on to him. There's an alarmed look on his face like he's been caught standing naked in the street. He spins back around to the gate and starts to try to slip through the small opening— but thankfully, Joe intervenes.

With a thunderclap of a bark, Joe positions himself squarely between Frederick and the gate, teeth bared. Frederick halts, startled by the wall of fur. He steps away from the gate, hands covered in drool. Beside him, Penny gasps.

"Joe!" Penny says to my dog, surprised to see him in such an aggressive stance. So far, she's only met his cuddly side.

"Going somewhere, Frederick?" I ask, trying to keep my voice even.

"How dare you address me so casually?! Get the mutt out of my way," Frederick snaps, but Joe growls, his stance unyielding.

"Good boy," I murmur, pride warming me. Joe stands as our majestic, immovable line of defense.

The commotion causes a crowd to start to gather around us. A circle of reporters forms a ring beside groups of villagers, their cameras pointed at us in accusation.

"Frederick," I begin, my voice surprisingly steady given the circus around us.

"You will address me as the Duke of Highland," he snarls.

"Even better," I nod. "Dearest Duke," I start again, pointing a finger at him. "Upon your arrival in the Village of Atwood, you went to gamble at the local casino. And you let slip a secret at the Blackjack table. You got drunk and blabbered to the dealer that you are the mastermind behind Highland's port chaos— you've been selling ship schedules to line your pockets and feed your gambling habit. Isn't that right?"

His face pales, turning a ghostly shade that could give the pastel buildings of Atwood Village a run for their money. "How could you— you couldn't possibly know—" He stammers.

"That's why you booked the impromptu trip to visit your cousin, the Duke of Atwood, here at the castle. You were trying to run from the mess you'd made at home. But you couldn't outrun the truth. In a moment of weakness, you let your secret slip to the Blackjack dealer. Then, when the dealer got chatty with Rodrigo about it, you silenced Rodrigo permanently." The accusation hangs heavy in the air. Murmurs ripple through the crowd. "Rodrigo was going to publish a story about your gambling problem, and the fact that you were selling secrets about our port schedules in Highland to cover your debts. That's why the title was *'The Crown Doesn't Belong on His Head.'* It was *your* head he was talking about! He was saying that you don't deserve a royal title!"

"How *dare* you!" Frederick protests, but his voice cracks in admission. "This is preposterous!

"Is it?" I press on, "Because Monrovian law is crystal clear. A Royal who commits treason or betrays their country can't hold a title. I read that in a little book I found at *Cafe de Flore*." I scan the crowd, noticing Jocelyn off to the side. She smiles at me, encouraging. "A book on Monrovian law. The same book in which you planted a handkerchief to frame the Duke of Atwood. You knew Officer Basilier was eager to blame him, and you hoped to frame him for what you did. You were reading the book on Monrovian law to try and find a loophole — a way out of the mess you'd created with the ports in Highland. When you realized you couldn't escape, you hid the handkerchief at the crime scene and called into Officer Basilier with an anonymous tip."

Maggie nods, her braids bouncing with the motion. "That's right! Monrovian law says those who commit treason are ineligible to hold Royal titles. Which means if you're found guilty of such a crime, the title of Duke of Highland would fall to—" She pauses dramatically, pointing towards Penny, "—to Penny!"

All eyes shift to Penultima, soon-to-be Duchess of Highland if all falls into place. She stands there, a mixture of shock and realization dawning like the morning sun over

Monrovia's coastal horizon. She turns to her brother, betrayed.

"Frederick," she says quietly. "Tell me you didn't?"

He doesn't answer her, and his silence seems to say it all.

"You were desperate to keep your title because it allows you to live a life of gambling and play. You were so desperate you were willing to frame the Duke of Atwood—"

My eyes scan the crowd for Jack, who seems to have just arrived. He's talking to Henri, the Baker, who's whispering in his ear. Given the look of betrayal on Jack's face, Henri has just told him the truth about his cousin.

"Cousin?" Jack says, his voice cracking. The crowd stares at him. "How could you? I asked you directly if you were responsible for the situation with the ports in Highland and you *lied* to my face!"

"I couldn't—" Frederick stammers. "I tried—"

"He did it because he can't stop gambling," My words tumble out, fueled by the thrill of solving a mystery not even the gossip rags saw coming. "And he didn't care who he hurt along the way. Not you— the Duke of Atwood. Not the people of Monrovia. Not even his own sister."

Frederick, now cornered and deflated, looks at each of us in turn, his shoulders slumping under the weight of our gazes. His desperate eyes scan the crowd, searching for an ally. Instead, he finds scorn. Conversation bubbles up among the villagers, and by the sound of it— they're outraged.

"The price of sugar!" Henri shouts. "The shortages are the fault of one of our Royals?!"

"My shipments of dog leashes have been delayed for weeks!" Benjamin echoes over the crowd.

"What does she know?" Frederick shouts over the commotion. "Are you all really going to believe her? She's not even one of us!" he spits out, voice laced with venom.

Before I can fashion a retort, Jocelyn stands up, her soft-spoken nature giving way to a rare fierceness. "Rebecca has shown us nothing but kindness and respect," she declares, the subtle floral scent of her *Cafe de Flore* lingering even here.

"*Oui*," agrees Benjamin, his green eyes alight. "She's more Monrovian than you'll ever be, *monsieur*. She embodies our spirit!"

"Rodrigo would have admired her sleuthing," Zacharia chimes in, earnest and eager as ever.

It's then that Henri steps forward. He nods solemnly, his stout frame a testament to his steadfastness. "I stand with Rebecca." He looks at me, an apology in his eyes. "She is a true Monrovian, valuing truth, tradition, and honesty." He moves closer to me and takes my hand, patting the top of it. Then, he says, just to me— "You are… a true Monrovian."

The moment seems to enrage Frederick. "Alright, yes!" he finally bursts out, his confession slicing through the tension. "I *killed* that terrible reporter," his face flushes crimson. "But none of you know what it is to be in my position. The pressure I am under!"

There's a collective gasp. Reporters shout questions into the air. Cameras flash. Frederick— the Duke of Highland— has issued a public confession. There's no going back now.

At the front of the crowd, Jack— having allowed the spectacle to unfold— now steps forward, every bit the Royal Frederick isn't. His silver hair glimmers, bringing a gravitas to his movements. He steps toward Officer Basilier, who's standing — shocked— at the edge of the crowd, her daughter beside her. "It seems you may have gotten your Royal criminal after all," he says, locking eyes with her. His tone is calm— collected— but beneath it lies an undercurrent of challenge. "The question now is... do you care about what's right? And— will you teach *her* what's right?" He glances down at Officer Basilier's daughter.

There's a pause, and for a moment I think Officer Basilier might refuse to take action. But then, to my surprise, she strides over to Frederick, cuffs in hand.

"Frederick Armistead— the Duke of Highland— you're under arrest for the murder of a citizen of the Village of Atwood," she states, her voice clear and unwavering. Reporters shout questions, but they don't get answers. Office Basilier leads Frederick away, his future uncertain— but whatever it is, it's definitely not one that involves a Royal title.

I exchange a look with Jack. There's a silent understanding that passes between us, a shared sense of relief and hope. I want to talk to him, but the crowd separates us. Reporters— unable to get a quote from Frederick— descend instead upon Jack, Penny, and… most surprisingly, *me*.

Cameras click and flash. The Duke, who has been a pillar of calm amid the chaos, fields questions from reporters who seem to pop up from the cobblestones.

"Your Grace, comments on the recent revelations? How does it feel to have your name cleared?" one reporter calls out, thrusting a microphone under his nose.

"Relieved," the Duke says, his voice steady and assured. "Relieved that the truth has come to light, thanks to Rebecca."

"Rebecca," another journalist turns to me, her pen poised like a fencer ready to strike, "did you ever doubt your instincts? Does being an animal trainer make you *more* in tune with your instincts?"

"No, instincts are Joe's job," I reply with a grin, nodding to Joe, who's lapping up attention from a group of children.

"Miss Penny!" A reporter breaks through the throng, aiming for Penny, who looks as if she'd rather be anywhere but here. "How does it feel to be the new Duchess of Highland?"

Penny, bless her, manages a brave smile despite the whirlwind around us. "I... I'm still processing it all," she admits, her voice barely rising above the din. "My brother has let the country down. But I am committed to serving Highland and Monrovia with all my heart." Despite her regal assurances, I can see the emotion in her eyes— Penny's heartbroken over Frederick's betrayal. But I know she won't let it stop her from serving the people.

As the crowd surges forward, I catch Penny's arm and pull her aside, away from the eager press and curious onlookers. Beside us, Maggie manages to squeeze her way through the throng. The three of us stand together, and I point across the courtyard to the statue Monrosha, bathed in the soft glow of the festival lights. She holds her basket, filled with bread, prepared to share with all who need it.

"Ladies," Maggie says. "We did this."

"Monrosha was a leader who rose above her circumstances," I say to Penny, feeling the connection between past and present. "She built something lasting, something good, out of adversity. That's what *you're* going to do for Highland."

"Thank you, Rebecca," Penny says, her voice both warm and strained. "I hope I can live up to that legacy."

We share a quiet moment, letting the noise of the festival fade into a background hum. I look back at the statue, feeling a sense of pride swelling within me—a pride for this country, for the friends I've made, and for the strength we all carry within us.

"History has a funny way of coming full circle," I muse. "Who knows? Maybe one day they'll put up a statue of you, Penny. Just make sure they get your good side."

Her laugh mingles with the festivities around us. And as we turn back to join the others, I know that whatever comes next, Monrovia is a place I belong.

CHAPTER
Nineteen

LATER, the festival is over, and the Castle grounds are quiet — almost *too* quiet. The last of the visitors have trickled away, leaving the echo of laughter and the scent of cotton candy clinging to the void. Joe and I walk through the courtyard, taking in the ghostly remains of the Foundation Festival. My boots crunch over a confetti patchwork of flyers and stray streamers. The once vibrant tents stand forlorn, like sentinels guarding memories of celebration, their colors muted in the twilight. A few staff members pick up the trash with long sticks and plastic bags, determined to right the wreckage of the day.

"Looks like the party ended when we weren't looking, huh?" I chuckle to Joe, who gives a lazy wag of his tail, his golden fur catching the fading sunlight. We've already herded the animals back into their cozy pens, and now we watch as workers dismantle the fence from the petting zoo, piece by clanking piece.

"Rebecca!" Maggie's voice cuts through the quiet, her braids bouncing as she trots toward me with her bright, reliable smile. "I just got off the phone with the King and Queen."

"Really?" I arch an eyebrow, brushing a strand of hair from my face. "And what did Monrovia's finest have to say?"

"They're over the moon! The case is solved, the Duke's name is cleared, and it's all thanks to you." She beams, hands on hips in a stance that says she's proud to know me.

"Aw, shucks," I say with mock humility, tipping an imaginary hat. "Just doing my part to keep Monrovia quirky and crime-free."

"They've put me on PR duty. Lots more calls to make." She glances past me, and her smile widens mischievously. "Speaking of calls to make, look who's heading our way."

I follow her gaze to see Jack approaching, his silver hair catching the waning light, a serious but warm look softening the lines around his eyes.

"Ah, I see," I nod, feeling the corners of my mouth tug upwards. "Well, I wouldn't want to keep royalty waiting."

"I have so many calls to take… I'll leave you two to talk," Maggie says, giving me a knowing wink before flitting away.

"Looks like you're a free man," I say to Jack as he reaches down to scratch Joe's ears. "How does it feel to no longer be labeled a criminal?"

"I kind of miss the edge to my reputation," the Duke smirks at me. "I think it gave me a certain allure that's lost now that I'm back to being the bookish Duke, I'm afraid."

"You could never lose your allure." The words slip out of my mouth with a frankness that makes us both blush.

"While that's entirely untrue, I'm certainly glad you think so," the Duke says. I can smell his cologne from here, and it's the kind of scent that stays with a person. One you want to lean into, like a warm hug. "I believe I owe you and Joe my life once more," he smiles at me. "It seems that your arrival in Monrovia was one of my luckiest days. I only want to thank you, and yet, I'm afraid our last dinner was too formal—"

"It was wonderful—"

"I'm afraid I went too far," he says, grinning. "I made the

evening too formal in my efforts to impress. You are a true Monrovian now, but the American love of the casual is something I hope you'll never lose. We met over bacon and a dog if you'll recall."

"Something I could never forget," I agree, thinking of the moment I met Jack on the plane, when Joe went to steal a piece of bacon from his plate.

"Perhaps, for our next meal, I could take you somewhere more casual. Where we're less..." Jack searches for the word. "... observed? And can be more of our true selves? It's difficult to pick a casual place in the village as I'm afraid I garner stares and observation everywhere I go, but perhaps Henri would close *Le Petit Scone* for an evening so we can have a private dinner."

"I like your true self," I say stupidly. *Pull it together, Rebecca,* I think. Something about the Duke makes me feel totally at home, but also tongue-tied. "I mean, I like *my* true self. Also. And I *am* American. And Monrovian. Which means I love scones. And I think Henri approves of me now."

"He does," Jack's smile grows. "That's a yes, then? To another meal together?"

"Yes," I nod enthusiastically. "An absolute yes."

"Good," Jack agrees. "We'll go immediately. I'll have Maggie schedule it as soon as possible. I don't want anything to get in the way." He sighs, looking weighed down with a heavy burden. "I'm afraid more relatives of mine are coming to town soon. And these ones are... particularly challenging." He issues the words in a mumble, as if he's speaking only to himself. "They insist on bringing the crown jewels into town, which will create such a ruckus, such a security burden— I shudder to think. We'll be responsible for hosting the jewels at the local museum. Poor Maggie and I will have our hands full. It's a planning nightmare."

"More royal relatives?" I can't help but cringe, imagining

the sort of high-maintenance, tiara-touting entourage that might descend upon our peaceful village.

"Yes," Jack offers a smirk and an apologetic grin. "But whatever trouble they bring, I'll be glad to know I have moments with you to look forward to." With that, he kisses my hand, his eyes lingering on mine just long enough to make me hold back a sigh. "Good night, Rebecca." He offers a final smile before crossing the courtyard and disappearing into the castle.

I look down at Joe, whose tail wags with a gentle sway. "More royal relatives coming into town, bud. How bad can they be?"

Joe's tail stops wagging and he looks up at me, eyes wide, as if to say— *why would you tempt fate by saying that out loud? Now they're going to be awful!* His reaction makes me laugh. Trust Joe to keep things in perspective. Still, whatever's coming for us, I know we can handle it— together.

As I walk back toward my apartment in the staff quarters, Joe plods along beside me. We pass that statue of Monrosha again. The staff hasn't taken it down yet, and she's still there, looking at me. We stop and admire her beauty, and I swear— just for a second— I think I see her smile at me.

———

For an excerpt from book three in the Rebecca Orange Castle Cozy Mystery series, keeping reading!

"A Royal Ruse"

EXCERPT

I kind of understand why people become monks, now, I think to myself as I take in the glinting stained glass windows of the rebuilt monastery that cradles me in its arms. I'm standing in an ancient building that used to house spiritual leaders, but that's now been renovated for a modern purpose. I appreciate that the building has been allowed to keep its original charm. Stone walls frame archways, butting up against firm, wooden doors with iron locks. It's a place that would be peaceful if it were currently filled with visitors.

I lean down to my dog, Joe— who's standing by my side — and scratch his enormous, golden head. He's dressed for the occasion, wearing a bandana that cascades down his chest. Its printed with the image of a suit on it, and when he sits down, he looks like he's in formal wear. "What do you think, bud?" I ask him. "Could *you* live in a monastery?"

"You already have a castle!" Maggie laughs beside me. "What more do you two want?" She pauses as a waiter comes by, holding a plate of hors d'oeuvres. She grabs a pastry wrapped in bacon off the plate and shoves it in her mouth, taking another sip of her wine. "I wish the Duke would start his speech already," she says, mouth full. "I have so much work to do for the grand opening—"

Just then, a crackling noise emerges from a platform that's been set up as a stage at the front of the monastery's enormous grand hall. In front of us, the entire village has assembled, eager townsfolk awaiting to hear what's planned for this building— straight from Jack, the Duke of Atwood. He stands at the microphone, arms open wide.

"Welcome," says the Duke. "I'm so glad you could all make it." Jack's voice makes my stomach fill with butterflies. I try to ignore them. Jack is my boss and falling in love with him is a terrible idea. *Keep it professional, Rebecca,* I think. To distract myself, I look around at the crowd that's assembled under the elaborate arches and exposed stonework. The entire town seems to have turned out.

"You are the very first to see the new Royal Heritage Museum!" The Duke continues proudly. "The monastery hasn't been used in hundreds of years, and we thought there was no better way to honor its history than to renovate the space and give it back to the people as a museum."

Typical Jack, I can't help but smile. He always wants to give back to the town and its residents— even when it costs him personally.

"In addition to displaying items from the Village of Atwood's history, I'm thrilled to announce that this museum will soon house the pride and joy of Monrovia's past..." Jack pauses for dramatic effect. "The Monrovian Crown Jewels."

Gasps emerge from the crowd. A ripple of excitement fills the hall. I turn to Maggie, who beams at me. She can tell by my expression I don't understand the excitement. "It's a very big deal, Rebecca," she whispers. "The Monrovian Crown Jewels are our most famous historical artifact. In their current home, they get as many visitors as the Tower of London! Bringing the jewels here is a huge honor for the village of Atwood."

"I'd like to offer special thanks to our museum curator, Dr. Lauda Remier, who recently graduated with her PhD from the Monrovian Institute, and has personally ensured our museum exhibitions live up to the highest of standards." The Duke motions to a woman standing of to the side of the stage. She's homely-looking, wearing a suit jacket and glasses, her dark hair pulled back into a tight bun. She waves at the crowd.

"Tonight, I'm pleased to show you the interior of the museum, and encourage you to take in our exhibits, including ancient Monrovian pottery," Jack continues, waving at the space. "Tomorrow morning, you'll all get a sneak preview of the Crown Jewels in the town square at a special event *just* for Atwood locals. Once the rest of the world knows, I'm afraid the museum will be packed with tourists, so I'd like to give the townsfolk first chance at seeing the gems." Murmurs of approval ripple through the room. "If everything goes as planned, the museum will bring millions of tourist dollars to the Village of Atwood, as well as to our small businesses here, like *Le Petit Scone,*" the Duke motions to the baker, Henri, who's standing at the front of the crown, still wearing his white chef's uniform. "Or *Cafe de Flore,*" Jack adds, waving to Jocelyn, the owner of my favorite cafe in town. "My hope is that every business in the village will see new opportunities for growth, given the increase in tourism brought by making Atwood the home of the Crown Jewels. But we can't do this without you," the Duke adds, meeting people's eyes. I see nods all around me— the townspeople are already sold on the idea. "The increase in visitors will mean changes in Atwood, but also new opportunity. And we're going to tackle it as we always do… together"."

As Jack's speech ends, the room erupts into thunderous applause. The crown returns to their snacks and mingling as Jack descends from the stage, shaking hands as he goes.

"He's really going all in," I whisper to Maggie. Joe is busy weaving between my legs, thrilled by the crowd and attention.

"He wants this more than anything," she says, squeezing my arm. "He really thinks it will give the economy here a boost. Looks like everyone thinks so, too."

I scan the room. There's Benjamin, the owner of *L'anima-lerie Indiana Bones* talking a mile a minute to a village, most likely about his favorite movies. Henri the baker looks especially pleased, like he knows exactly how many pastries this will sell. Jocelyn and Zachariah— the new owner of the gossip magazine stand— are leaning toward each other, deep in conversation. At the far end of the room, I see Castle Atwood staff standing in a circle, looking thrilled at the news. Everyone seems swept up by the announcement.

Maggie leans closer. "There she is," she says, nodding to the stage. I spot a young woman in towering heels and trendy clothes, barely containing her boredom. She shakes Jack's hand as he walks off the stage, but looks like she'd rather be anywhere else. "Lady Henrietta Grendana," Maggie explains. "And the little one next to her is her lady in waiting, Bitty. They've been awful guests at the castle. Poor Monique had to clean their room three times until it was to their liking, and Enrique's exhausted from driving them all around town." I glance back at the Castle Atwood staff, and notice that Monique and Enrique *do* look particularly exhausted.

Just then, the Duke approaches us, and time seems to slow down as he walks toward me. *Try to look like a normal human being, Rebecca,* I say to myself. *Close your mouth. Don't hold it open like a trout.* I shut my mouth and swirl my drink in its glass, offering the Duke a soft smile. I hate that I've grown to like my boss so much, but funny enough, it's for all the right reasons. I don't care about his Royal title or family money. I just like the way he spends nights and the library, and the crinkle in his smile.

"Do you two think it went well?" The Duke asks Maggie and I in a hushed tone, glancing around the room.

"They loved it," I assure him. "That was some speech you made."

"This is going to change *everything*," Maggie says, jumping up and down. "Atwood is going to be busier than ever this summer."

"*Oui*," a gruff voice says over Maggie's shoulder. It belongs to the baker, Henri, who's as close to 'happy' as I've ever seen him. Henri doesn't smile much, but there's crumbs in his bear, and his eyes are lit up. "I may finally be able to hire more help," he says. "No more hand-rolling croissants for me."

The Duke puts a hand on Henri's shoulder as if they're old friends. "Henri has promised me a small favor. Actually, it's a favor for you *and* me, Rebecca," he adds, the slightest flush coloring his cheeks.

"Yes, yes," Henri says, waving a hand in the air. "*Le Petit Scone* is yours for an evening. I will keep the staff late. Draw the blinds. No one will be the wiser."

My heart pounds in my chest. I was sure the Duke had forgotten the dinner he'd promised, but here he is, arranging everything. Whenever I think he's forgotten all about me, he proves otherwise.

"This weekend, Rebecca. You and me. A night with no crowds and no interruptions. What do you say?" Jacks smiles at me.

"Only if Joe can come," I say stupidly, acting as if my dog is an emotional support anima.

"I wouldn't expect anything different," Jack agrees. Then, he looks around the room. "Where *is* the little rascal? I would expect him to be here in full regalia."

I glance down, realizing Joe has disappeared. Then, a hand waves at me from the other side of the grand hall. It's

Benjamin, and he's feeding Joe snacks from off his plate. He points to Joe's outfit and gives me a thumbs up. We bought the attire from Benjamin's store, and it seems as if he approves.

"I'd better get back to my guests," the Duke says, look back at Lady Henrietta, who's still standing by the stage. "I don't know if Maggie's told you but they're..."

"Evil—" Maggie interjects.

"*Difficult*," the Duke corrects. "Rebecca, I look forward to this weekend."

The Duke offers a polite kiss on my hand before heading back toward the stage. Maggie offers me a knowing smirk.

"Don't say a word—" I caution her.

"Wasn't going to!"

"Royalty and—" Henri says, scanning me head to toe. "And ordinary person? What can it be?"

"Henri!" Maggi says, slapping his arm.

"I know, I know," I say, familiar with Henri's prejudice. "I'm American and I couldn't possibly understand."

"*Non*, it's not that you are American," Henri says, shaking his head. "It's that you are as ordinary as Maggie and me. These Royals, they live in a different world." He points at the Duke, who's standing beside Lady Henrietta, both of them looking other-worldly in their formal attire. "They are groomed for the crown. They can never understand the ordinary person, nor can an ordinary person understand them. You work with animals, yes? Then you must know, a bird and a fish can never be."

"That's great Henri," Maggie says, rolling her eyes. "But we have to stop Rebecca's dog from eating ice out of that champagne bucket."

"Blame me if you must," Henri says, throwing his hands in the air. "But I am only speaking the truth. Look at how the crown jewels came to be. Even when the commoner has money, it does not matter— love cannot overcome all."

"Thanks for the pep talk, but we'll be going now!" Maggie says. She grabs my elbow and pulls me across the room. Henri's voice echoes in my ears. *A bird and a fish can never be.* It's never occurred to me before that my lack of Royal status might be a problem in dating the Duke. I'd been so obsessed with the idea he's my boss, it hadn't even hit me we might have a bigger problem— he's Royal. And I'm— just Rebecca Orange.

"Rebecca," Maggie clucks at me, shaking her head. She can see the pain that's etched in my eyes. "Henri is an idiot. We keep him around because he makes amazing croissants, but he's an idiot with outdated ideas. Don't let him get to you."

"But what if he's right?"

"He's *never* right," Maggie sighs. "Unless it comes to bread. He once told me I was improper for using the castle SUV to pickup my breakfast and that it should be for Royals only. I was so mad I almost revoked his business license, but that I remembered that little bread he makes with the golden raisins. You know that one?"

"I love that one," I agree.

"And I just couldn't do it," she sighs. "I *need* that bread. But the point is— don't listen to anything Henri says.

She pulls me toward Joe, who— as Maggie correctly pointed out— has gotten into the ice box under the bar, where bottles of champagne are being kept. I grab him by the collar and he emerges, chewing a giant ice cube and crunching it right in front of me. "Joe," I laugh. "You are the world's *worst, best*-trained dog."

His eyebrows arch at me, softening the sting of our exchange with Henri. Still, the idea's been planted, and I wonder once again if our upcoming dinner is really a date, or just a warm friendship. Even if it *is* a date, maybe the Duke only sees me as someone to bide the time with, rather than someone to love.

"I think I might call it a night," I say to Maggie, secretly hoping to get back to my apartment at the castle and dip into my giant bathtub.

"Me too," Maggie yawns, checking her watch. "I've got so much to do tomorrow.

The three of us move to leave together, making our way toward the entrance. The old monastery doors are thrown wide open. A gentle breeze carries the sound of festivities into the evening. Just as I think we might escape, Joe puts on the brakes. He's focused on a tall man standing just outside the doorway. The man's got a gun at his side, but Joe's far more interested in the snack peeking from his pocket. He drags me over to investigate. "Looks like someone needs a treat," the man says in a thick Monrovian accent, offering a chunk of pastry to my giant dog. "Or maybe you are looking for a job?"

The man's grinning, broad and muscular with the air of someone who doesn't scare easily. He holds out a hand in greeting, and I shake it. "I'm Anthony, with the royal guard."

"Anthony's in charge of protecting the jewels," Maggie says. "The Royal Family sent him specifically to look after them."

"I could use some help, though," Anthony smiles at Joe. "Any chance your dog would want to join me as backup?"

"Trust me, you don't want him," I laugh. "If a jewel thief offers him some bacon, those gems are gone."

Anthony offers a hearty laugh as we depart, waving at us as we head down the steps. The night air is brisk and cool. The monastery is located on the edge of the village near a peaceful road. The cobblestones click under my feet as the moon lights the way. Then, the silence is interrupted by a woman's voice.

We *hear* the protestor before we see her, and I can just make out the sign in her hand. "Keep your jewels! Royals are wrong!" She shouts her chant against the night, her figure pacing in place as a lone bastion to her cause. "Royals are wrong! Royals are wrong!"

"Oh *no*," Maggie lets out a low whistler. "Well, at least it's only one."

We approach the protestor, and I get a better look at her under the light escaping through the open monastery doors. She's a young woman in her early twenties with with hair as blue as her outrage. She's holding a sign above her head, but she sets it down on our approach, and grabs a pamphlet out of her pocket. "Take one?" she asks.

"What exactly are you protesting?" I say, grabbing the pamphlet and opening it up to find a picture of the Royal Family within.

"The crown jewels are a symbol of monarchical oppression," the woman says passionately.

"Thanks but no thanks," Maggie rolls her eyes. "That monarchical oppression pays *both* our salaries." Maggie proceeds to continue her walk down the cobblestone path, and Joe and I follow her.

"If you change your mind, my email is on there!" The woman shouts behind us. "Pepper dot anarchist!"

"Pepper dot anarchist?" I whisper to Maggie under my breath, laughing. "Our big opposition is one girl named pepper who doesn't believe in any sort of government at all?"

"At least it's not an angry mob," Maggie agrees. "I just hope she's not at the grand unveiling of the jewels tomorrow. We really need this to go to smoothly. The Duke, the castle, the village... we're all counting on this to go well."

"Maggie," I say, shaking my head. "It's *us*. When do we ever find things go smoothly?

Maggie laughs and— with perfect timing— Joe lets out an enormous sigh, as if he's certain trouble is just on the horizon and even the idea of it is exhausting him. I scratch his ears, bending down to his level.

"What do you think, bud? Will things go smoothly tomorrow?" I ask him.

His big, soft eyes say no. And a glance back at Pepper— still marching in place— tells me he's right.

———

To continue the adventure, order book three in the Rebecca Orange Castle Cozy Mystery Series, "A Royal Ruse," available now!

Dear Reader,

Thank you for dedicating your time to the world of Monrovia and Rebecca Orange! These books mean so much to me, and my hope is always that what I've written gives you the chance to escape to a cozy new place.

I love hearing from readers (seriously, it makes the job so fun!). Please reach out to me anytime by visiting www.valeriebrandy.com or finding me on social media, even if it's just to say "hi" or talk about flower names for coffees. Monrovia is special because of the community there, and I love forming the same cozy friendships around my books.

You can also join my author club mailing list for free giveaways and updates on new releases.

Warmly,

— Valerie Brandy